MISS MARY

MISS MARY

THE LEGEND OF MISS MARY MACK

KATHBELL STUMPF

KenzieMac Publishing LLC

To all the inspirational females in my life

PROLOGUE

The room was dark except for a small glow radiating from two red metal lanterns. The four high school students sat on the wooden floor, which was coated in a light film of dust and stains from centuries past. The dampness in the historic home's walls filled the air with a pungent moldy odor that mixed with the overwhelming ashy scent from the large stone fireplace. Two girls sat facing each other anxiously. "You ready?" Caroline asked, raising her eyebrows at Rebecca.

"God this is sooo creepy! I guess... let's just get started." She shuddered as shivers ran down her back.

The two girls began by crossing their arms across their chests, then unfolded them and clapped their hands together. Then they crossed each hand, one at a time, and slapped each other's hands together, followed by this motion again with the opposite hand. While doing this, they sang the old rhyme.

"Miss Mary Mack Mack Mack
All dressed in black, black, black
With silver buttons, buttons, buttons
All down her back, back, bah—"

Corey, Rebecca's boyfriend, abruptly interrupted the rhyme. "Holy crap! Do you guys hear that?!" he exclaimed nervously as his eyes darted around the room, seeking for something he couldn't visibly see lying deep in the shadows of the old house.

CHAPTER ONE

Anna sat in Algebra II staring at the blackboard attempting to force herself to focus on what Mr. Hall was trying to teach. She opened her eyes wider in the hopes that she would feel more awake. Anna struggled with sleeping the night before, tossing and turning as severe storms boomed thunder and flashed lightning through most of the autumn night until the early hours of the morning. The weather during class didn't help as thick gray clouds covered the sky outside, making it a very dull day with hardly any light coming through the four big windows in the room. Her sleepy thoughts were interrupted when she heard the slow, tap... tap... tap... of a pen hitting a tabletop.

She looked over to her left to see Boston looking directly at her. As she followed his hand up to meet his face, he gave her a slight grin. Her heart jumped with excitement as she shyly turned her head away to face the blackboard again. *OMG, OMG, was he just intentionally trying to get my attention? He is SO freakin' hot!*

Boston's medium-brown hair with honey tones shined under the fluorescent lights above him. His hair had just enough product to make it look messy but neat. His big brown eyes burned into Anna's suggestively. His strong muscular face, lightly tanned skin, and elongated straight nose reminded her of a Greek gladiator. His broad shoulders and tall athletic build made him a natural-born football player.

Shortly thereafter, the bell rang. Everyone closed their books and jumped up from their seats. Abbey walked over to Anna's desk; "Ugh this rainy dull day is making me just want to go home and climb into bed with a good Audible."

"Oh, I know exactly how you feel. I could have just fallen asleep during that class," Anna said, putting her algebra book and MacBook Air back into her backpack. The girls slowly strolled out of the classroom and into the hallway.

"Don't forget, guys and gals, quiz next Monday. So, make sure you read through chapters nine and ten!" shouted Mr. Hall as students continued to file out of his classroom door.

"I have zero desire to read through those on my weekend. I would rather watch paint dry!" Anna said through a big, sleepy yawn.

"Ha! Ditto!" replied Abbey. "So, I couldn't help but notice you and Boston swapping smiles or, dare I say, sharing a moment. You guys just need to quit flirting around the issue and get together already. Just ask him out, Anna; he obviously likes you!" Abbey insisted as Anna opened her locker door.

Cannon Falls High stood on top of one of the largest hills in town, viewable from the main street and town square below. Perched up high, the gothic architecture served as tribute to those who have graduated over the past 200 years and as a constant reminder of the Monday morning bell for its current students. Being an old school, the beautiful big gray stone slabs, the rooftop's many peaks, and the turret windows oozed with charm. Everything was beautiful about the old building except for the off-colored orange lockers lining all three levels of hallways which left a lot to be desired. Glass cases ran along the walls of the main floor hallway, enclosing football trophies dating back to the early 1900s. Cannon Falls is extremely proud of its Civil War history and everything that came after it that makes Cannon Falls such a safe and picturesque place to live and grow up.

The football team, the 'Napoleons,' have been undefeated for the past three years and nobody in town forgets that. The team has a history of consecutive periods of time in which the football team goes undefeated for season after season, making them one of the teams to beat in the great state of Pennsylvania. The high school's team mascot of the Napoleons was named after one of the most popular cannons used during the Civil War since the town of Cannon Falls was a big producer and supplier of the required iron cannon balls.

"Abbey, you are out of your mind if you think that I am going to ask Boston Tate out! Nobody on our celebrity football team would be interested in me. I'm nobody to them. He was just being nice. He's just a nice guy!" exclaimed Anna in complete rebellion to Abbey's idea.

"Whatevs, Anna. I guess that's why he goes out of his way to stop by our lunch table on an almost daily basis to say 'hi' to you. But fine, if you're too much of a wuss to do it, then don't," Abbey responded in annoyance.

"Anyway, if he really did like me, then he would just ask me out, like a real gentleman should," snorted Anna.

"Hmm, is that right?!" a voice beamed from behind Anna. Her face dropped with embarrassment; her eyes widened like saucers as she swallowed. Abbey just grinned with amusement. "So—you believe it's up to the guy to ask the girl out, huh? Isn't that a little old-fashioned of you, Anna? Here I thought you were a modern independent woman," Boston joked as a huge grin crept across his face.

Anna coughed to clear her throat and to buy herself a few extra seconds to think of a response. "Ummm, what did you think you heard, exactly?" Anna raised her eyebrows nervously.

"Just the part about the guy's role in the dating arena. Sooo... who's the guy you're talking about?" Boston asked inquisitively, his eyes burning into Anna's.

"Oh, no one. Abbey and I were just joking around. No one in particular, just... you know... girl talk." Anna beamed back, relieved with her quick comeback abilities. The bell rang down the school hallway; "One more class to go!" Anna said while slamming her locker door shut. With that, she walked off down the hall to art class, leaving Abbey and Boston to fend for themselves. *Phew, that was close. That could have been extremely embarrassing,* Anna thought to herself. *But seriously, why does Boston have to be so ridiculously gorgeous?!!*

During art class, Mrs. Abbott talked about Van Gogh and the love affairs that made him cut off his own ear. "Geez, what a nut job!" Jay whispered under his breath.

"Yeah, artistically brilliant, but fifty shades of nuts," Anna quietly giggled.

Jay had known Anna since they were in kindergarten together; he lived a few houses up the street from her and was the brother that Anna never had. There was a moment in time during freshman year when Anna thought Jay was beginning to develop feelings for her that went beyond their friendship. Jay for sure turned heads at school with his desirable tall, dark, and handsome look. Jay had a golden-brown complexion, chiseled jaw, large almond-shaped brown eyes, and broad shoulders. Jay was popular in his own right at school with his charismatic and outgoing attitude. It's hard to find someone at school that Jay doesn't know and talk to. Anna just found it too weird to imagine dating him, as her affection for him was way too platonic to be anything more.

Jay couldn't be blamed though. Anna was a very pretty girl with brownish-golden wavy hair that hung a couple of inches below her shoulders and a slim, curvaceous figure that did not go unnoticed by her classmates at school. Her intelligent, fun personality and good heart matched the exterior. Anna wasn't, however, the typical glamorous girl with five pounds of perfectly crafted makeup and a skirt four inches above her knees; she was naturally beautiful without having to try so hard. The first thing most people notice about Anna is her piercing green eyes, perfectly arched eyebrows, and full reddish lips. Anna was a sensible, fashionable girl who didn't try too hard with her clothing choices, not like Brianna and her pack of Barbie doll girlfriends. Anna was an only child. So she was always thankful to have Jay and Abbey both living nearby, as she never had to feel bored.

The final ring of the school bell chimed loudly at the end of art class, announcing the end of the school week just as thunder clapped outside. "Perfect," Anna shrugged as she looked over at Jay.

"Good thing you can drive us home now," replied Jay with a cheeky grin. Anna just got her license a few months ago but this was the first week that her parents let her drive to school. Anna turned seventeen on August 1st and her parents had bought her a 2017 Jeep Cherokee Latitude, white with black leather interior. Anna couldn't believe her luck; it was like brand new with a little over 45,000 miles on it.

Jay, Anna, and Abbey met up in the hallway by Anna's locker and made their way toward the large double doors of the school's main entrance, headed for Anna's car. Students were running frantically as the rain pelted down like an Amazonian monsoon, some with umbrellas and some using their backpacks, coats, or notebooks held above their heads to protect themselves from the downpour. As Anna got into her car, she realized that she had forgotten her Algebra II book in her locker. "Ugh, dang it! I forgot one of my freakin' textbooks!" she said while hitting the steering wheel with the palm of her hand.

"Do you really need it?" asked Jay.

"Yes, I have an Algebra II quiz to study for over the weekend... ugh! I'll be back in a minute."

"Here, take this," Abbey said while handing her a pink umbrella.

"Thanks! Won't be long!" Anna said, jumping out of her car door and into the rain.

As Anna walked toward the main entrance for the second time after retrieving her book, she heard Boston calling her name from behind her. "Anna Ipswich, wait up!" he shouted.

"Oh, hey Boston! What's up?" she replied as her stomach nerves buzzed like her cell phone on vibrate.

"So... I've been thinking, you must know by now that I'm interested in you, as in really interested, more than a friend?" he asked with a slanted, sexy grin as he raised his eyebrows. Before Anna could answer, he continued, "So anyway, my point is, I would really like to take you out one night on a date," Boston said confidently but without arrogance.

Holy shhhh! Anna was taken aback. Deep down she had an inkling that he might be interested in her but never dreamed that he would actually ask her out on a date. They didn't really run in the same circles. Beaming with excitement yet trying to play it cool, she responded, "Yeah, sure, why not?!" Anna danced circles in her head like a little child who just got a new toy that she's been wanting for Christmas.

"Great! Do you have any plans this Saturday?"

"Actually, I am going to the movies with some friends," she replied anxiously while rubbing her lips together.

"What about... What about Sunday? Lunch then a movie?" he asked, shrugging his shoulders with his hands in his pockets.

"There are a couple of movies out right now that I want to see. So that would be great," Anna replied reassuringly.

"Awesome!" What about the new Halloween movie? If you like horror, that is?"

"Yes. Cool, I love a good horror movie," Anna's smile beamed.

"Okay, well how about we have lunch at Fridays before the movie? I'll text you over the weekend to figure out what time I should pick you up Sunday." Now Boston was the one with a huge smile across his face and not doing such a great job at trying to conceal his excitement.

"Sounds perfect! I better go... my friends are waiting in my car for a ride home," she laughed.

"Cool. Just let me get your number, and you'll also need to text me your address," Boston replied.

As Anna returned to her SUV and climbed into the driver's seat, she was buzzing with excitement.

"God... what's gotten into you all of a sudden?" asked Jay.

"Yeah, give it up, Anna!" egged on Abbey.

"Well... I just bumped into Boston in the hallway, and he asked me out on a date! Oh-my-god! I am going out on a date with Boston on Sunday, wahoo!!" she exclaimed.

"Yes!! Anna, that's amazing!" Abbey shouted back.

"Ladies, can you please both stop shrieking? Jesus!" Jay demanded.

"Shut up, Jay! Get over it. Anna deserves to be excited. Don't be such a buzz kill," Abbey snorted.

"Yeah, be quiet Jay. Let me enjoy this moment," Anna giggled.

Jay rolled his eyes; "Girls," he laughed out loud while flicking on the radio. "Ah! Finally, some testosterone... I was afraid I was turning into a girl," he said as Imagine Dragons played in the background.

Anna pulled up to her large white modern farmhouse-style home excited to tell her mom the great news. Anna had a very close relationship with her mom and dad, but with her mom, in particular. She felt like she could tell her mom anything. They would often hang out and watch movies at home together, go shopping, or go for a manicure and pedicure. She couldn't imagine ever moving away to college and being so far from them. One of the main reasons Anna planned on going to Penn State or The University of Gettysburg was so she could just stay at home or be within a short driving distance to her family.

Anna burst in the front door; "Mom! Mom! Where are you?" she shouted.

"In the kitchen with Dad, Anna!" her mom shouted back. Anna threw her backpack down by the stairs in the front entrance foyer.

"Hey Tutu! Hey Shaggy!" she said while rubbing both dogs on the head. "Such good puppies." Tutu was a little white Corgipoo with an extra fluffy butt that looked like she was wearing a white tutu, and Shaggy was a big black retriever whose hair was a little on the wild side.

"Hey hon... how was school?" Anna's mom asked while giving her a hug.

"The best day ever!"

"Oh, okay... tell us more!" inquired her dad as he threw a potato chip in his mouth and smiled.

"Hey Dad"; Anna smiled sweetly.

"Well, I got asked out today by Boston Tate, and we are going out on a date on Sunday! Lunch and a movie; I assume that's okay with you guys, right?" she said, grinning with a mouth full of teeth.

"Hah! You look like a Cheshire cat, Anna," her mom giggled. "I think that would be okay, right Dad?" her mom said while raising her eyebrows.

"Ummm... yeah, should be okay. I want to meet him first,

though. Just so I can check this guy out," her dad said with mixed emotions of amusement and concern.

"Sure, course!" Anna smiled.

"Oh honey, I'm so excited for you. I must say, he is a very good-looking young man, and I've heard he's a nice boy," her mom said while squeezing Anna's hand.

"I know, he really is. Oh, by the way, Abbey and Jay are coming over after we go out to eat at Eddie's Diner tonight."

"No problem... do you still want to go for a mani-pedi tomorrow?" her mom asked.

"Definitely!" Anna replied.

"Okay, I'm going to go get changed. Then I'll need to leave to go pick them up," Anna said while making her way out of the kitchen.

Abbey came running out of the house the moment Anna pulled up in her driveway. "Hey!" she said while closing the door. "I am starving! I hope Eddie's isn't too packed," she added while slouching into the seat.

Eddie's was one of the popular places to go Friday and Saturday nights. Everyone was there: the jocks... nerds... goths... all groups of people. It was a fifties style diner but with a modern twist. Eddie's had the best burgers in town and the most comprehensive jukebox ever. "So, Anna, what are you going to wear on Sunday, hmmm??"

Abbey arched one eyebrow up as the group planted down into the booth at Eddie's.

"I have no idea. I will figure it out tomorrow or Sunday. I don't want to overthink it."

"Anyway, what are you girls eating?" interrupted Jay.

"What else? Cheeseburger with fries and a strawberry shake," replied Anna.

"You?" she posed back to him.

"Triple burger, onion rings, beans, and a chocolate shake," Jay said before licking his lips.

"I'm going for a plain grilled chicken salad," Abbey said while bursting out into laughter. Abbey was built like a twig, naturally very skinny even though she ate like a horse. Her long blonde hair fell into curls. She was also modest with her makeup. Abbey had always been ambitious, a girl who was not afraid of anything. Naturally self-assured, she always pushed Anna to be more confident. She annoyed Jay at times, but she would do that on purpose; they fought like brother and sister sometimes. Abbey was also a very smart girl, who had been gunning to attend Brown University or NYU, and with her drive, Abbey would do anything she could to make sure that she got accepted.

"Good lord! Could their shorts seriously get any shorter? So redic!" hissed Abbey as Brianna and her four besties walked into the diner wearing four-inch stilettos. They never stay at Eddie's for longer than 30 minutes but have the ego to feel that it's their duty to make an appearance. As if every high school student's weekend night depended on Brianna showing off her latest new outfit. Typically, Brianna and her crew would be cheering at the football game on a Friday night, but this particular week was a bye week, so the team didn't have a game.

"Pathetic. It's totally desperate, but typical for that group," said Anna.

"I don't mind," laughed Jay with a wink.

"Well of course you would think that, perve," Abbey said while nudging Jay in the ribs.

"Wait a minute... she's looking over here at you, Anna. Ugh, they're coming over. God, what the heck does she want?" Abbey rolled her eyes in frustration.

"Hi guys!" Brianna said sarcastically with a fake smile.

"Brianna," hissed Abbey.

"Hi," Anna said inquisitively. Brianna and her group don't normally speak to anyone outside of their circle. They simply just don't care about anyone else. Except of course at prom time, or at a school event where people might be voting for Brianna, or if she's selling something.

"Hey Jay," Brianna smiled, pursing her overly glossed lips.

"What's up?" he replied while looking down at his iPhone. Jay is not impressed by Brianna or her friends. And in some strange way, it bugs the heck out of Brianna, as she is not used to guys ignoring her; they typically trip all over their feet for her.

"Sooo, Anna... a little birdy told me that you and Boston are going out on a date this Sunday. That was nice of him to take you out. I mean, he's such a friendly, caring person," Brianna said with a condescending tone.

"Yep... looking forward to it," Anna replied coolly. Abbey winked at Anna in support.

"Run along, ladies. I think that girl over there is wearing the same skirt as you, Brianna. You might want to go home and change. I know you don't want to end up on the 'Who wore it better?' list," Jay said, pointing to the twelve-year-old girl.

"Ha... ha... good one, Jay," snorted Abbey.

"Ugh, whatever... loser," Brianna huffed as they walked away.

"Thanks guys. Ugh, she's so rude. I really hope Boston wouldn't expect me to ever hang out with her if we start dating each other," Anna said sadly.

"You'll be fine. Just focus on having a great time with him. He's so nice. I don't understand why he's friends with her," Abbey chimed in with her support.

CHAPTER TWO

"Hmm, pink please - like that electric pink polish, please?" Anna requested to the woman at the nail salon. "Thanks for the mani-pedi, Mom," Anna said with a smile.

"So, honey... have you figured out what you are wearing for your date tomorrow?"

"Not yet. I haven't looked, to be honest," Anna replied as she sat back in the pedicure chair and pressed her feet into the warm pool of water.

"Good idea... you don't want to be too eager," laughed Anna's mom.

"Although there is one thing that makes me nervous about dating Boston; some of his friends aren't exactly friendly," sighed Anna.

"Oh, high school girls can be very jealous and very mean, honey. Did something happen to make you say that?"

"Well, Brianna was at Eddie's last night with her 'crew,' and she came over to my table and made some snarky comment about Boston going out with me. Basically, she was implying that Boston was going out on a date with me because he was a nice guy and felt sorry for me," Anna said while staring at the Civil War memorial statue in the town square through the spa's massive front window which, coincidentally, was great for people-watching.

"Lord. Well, just ignore her; she's obviously just jealous that you're going out with him. Don't let her ruin your date, or worse, drive a wedge between you and this nice boy," her mom replied assertively.

The Civil War statue in the Cannon Falls town square was built in 1903 as a memorial to the fallen Union soldiers. It depicted three soldiers loading a cannonball into a giant Napoleon cannon during battle. The men's uniforms look ragged with rips and tears; one man had a bandage across his head, and another had a deep cut on his hand. It was designed to show the valor, bravery, and perseverance of the soldiers.

Cannon Falls was named after the town's major contribution of producing cannon balls used by the Union Army during the Civil War. The town had its own scars from a major battle that took place when a group of Confederate troops tried to stop the production of the cannon balls. Located 40 miles north of Gettysburg, the two cities shared common stories of war-torn bloodshed. Cannon Falls' Main Street, made up of all historic buildings and cobblestone roads, is now a hot spot for boutique shopping, cafes, restaurants, and bars. The town square streets are lit constantly by multiple gas lamps which, per the Cannon Falls Historical Society, must stay lit 24 hours a day, 7 days a week. A small center stage gazebo was used during fall, spring, and summer months for concerts and festivals held by the city council. People would flock to listen to bands play, eat local food, and drink the local craft beer and wine.

The city was a decent size with a population of 80,000 people but had a quaint, small-town community feel. Everyone appreciates the history that is ever-present in every little crack of the pavement. The Historical Society worked hard to preserve the city's authenticity. The locals always said that the young can't wait to get out but also can't wait to come back to raise their children in a great, safe place where everyone takes care of each other. The hills surrounding the city's valley are draped with an eerie morning mist that dissipates as soon as the sun comes up high enough to banish the clouds away.

Anna looked down at her iPhone as she felt it vibrate in her coat pocket. It was a text message from Boston, *"Hi Anna. Pick you up at 12 tomorrow? Looking forward to it :)"*

Anna's stomach did a flip-flop as she unlocked her phone and sent a reply, *"Sounds good. See you then!"*

On Saturday night, Anna picked up Abbey, Jay, and Jay's friend, Alex, and headed out to the movies. "Yum... I'm so excited for popcorn and a slushy!" Abbey exclaimed.

"Are you going to be nice and share some of your popcorn with me this time?" Alex asked Abbey.

"If you're nice, maybe," she replied with a flirtatious tone and smirk. Abbey had had a thing for Alex for the past six months but kept wavering on the idea of dating him. He obviously wanted to ask her out, but she had concerns about it not working out and ruining their friendship or, particularly, the group dynamic.

Abbey is wise beyond her years, an old soul, as some might say; an old soul who has mastered the art of flirtation. Anna and Jay had taken bets on how long it will be until they finally give in and go on a date. Anna's guess was a couple more months, unless Abbey met someone else first, but Jay thought it would be a couple of weeks at the most.

During the movie, Anna couldn't seem to concentrate on anything except for her excitement about her date the next day. Her stomach did a somersault every time she thought about seeing Boston. Scenarios ran through her mind: him coming into her house and meeting her parents, riding in his car with him and listening to music together, sitting in a dark theater so close to each other; Anna fell into another daydream and her eyes glazed over.

"You're not enjoying the movie, Anna?" Jay whispered.

"No, it's okay. I'm just having trouble concentrating," Anna shook her head.

"You look as if you're majorly zoning out," Jay laughed.

"Just thinking about stuff, that's all. Abbey and Alex seem to be cozy," Anna said, leaning forward to peek.

"Ha ha, yep! No surprise there," Jay laughed.

On the way home, the foursome listened to Mumford and Sons on the radio. Alex and Abbey sat together in the back seat arguing whether the movie plot was stupid or not. Jay sat in the passenger seat playing with his phone, as usual.

"So, lemme guess, you're getting nervous for your date tomorrow with the infamous Boston?"

"I wouldn't say nervous... just excited and a little anxious for tomorrow to get here," she replied slowly while focusing on the thin country road surrounded by pitch-black air with no sign of any streetlights. The three-mile stretch of winding country roads led to Anna's subdivision. If Anna hadn't turned into her subdivision from State Road 106, she would have ended up taking the back route to Gettysburg, or what she referred to as the 'the booney way' to Gettysburg.

Anna looked down for a split second to change the radio station and suddenly heard Alex shout, "Anna! Holy shit look out!!"

"What a freakin' idiot!" Jay scoffed. As Anna looked up, a pair of headlights was swerving into her lane, facing her head-on. Luckily, the driver regained control of the vehicle and dragged it back into its own lane.

"Oh my god, I'm so sorry guys. That was so scary; he came out of nowhere!" said Anna apologetically.

"Phew! No worries, Anna. The car just came bounding round that corner, driving so erratically. What a jerk! Probably some idiot drunk driver or some moron from our school texting while driving," snorted Abbey.

"Gosh! That was really close," Anna replied, gripping the steering wheel tightly as her hands tingled with nerves. "Thank God you shouted, Alex. I shouldn't have been messing with the radio station. Lesson learned." It had really shaken Anna as it was her first experience with a potential driving hazard like that. Sensing her anxiety, Jay patted her on the shoulder.

"Chill, Anna. It's okay. We're totally fine," Jay said, reaching his arm over and gently squeezing her shoulder. "Did anyone happen to see what car that was or who was in it?"

"Well, it is pitch-black, Jay, so I don't know how anyone could have," Abbey replied sarcastically.

"Actually, Jay, there were four people in the car. I saw them as they drove past. They didn't look much older than us, but I can't be sure," Alex confirmed.

Everyone was finally dropped off at their homes safe and sound, including Anna, who kicked off her shoes by the front door while closing the door behind her. After grabbing a glass of water, she tip-toed past her dad who was sleeping on the couch in the living room (as usual) and headed upstairs to her bedroom. The last thought that ran through her mind was about her date with Boston the next day, which left a smile on her face a mile wide as she fell asleep.

The next morning Anna woke up extra early. The grin from the night before remained on her face. The first thought that popped into her head was, *What the heck am I going to wear?* She would finally allow herself to give it some thought. *I've got to do something to get rid of these butterflies... it's too early for this!*

With that, Anna jumped out of bed, pulled her hair back into a ponytail, pulled on her beanie cap, and threw on her black sweatpants with a long-sleeved workout top. She grabbed a bottle of water from the fridge and retrieved the leashes from the hallway closet. "Tutu! Shaggy! Walkies... let's go!" she shouted. Tutu and Shaggy came belting down the stairs to meet her in the entrance foyer. "Good puppies!" she said as she clipped the leashes onto their collars. After letting the dogs take a quick drink of water, she headed out the front door.

Anna faced the cool and refreshing fall breeze. Dried leaves skipped around the path beneath her feet. She loved nothing better than the crispness of a fall day. Anna made her way out of her subdivision and walked across the road to the park. The historic park was an old battleground dating back to the 1860s consisting of five different trails that ranged from 1.5 miles to 8 miles.

As she crossed the street, she shuddered thinking about the car from the night before that nearly hit her and her friends. "Idiot," she murmured under her breath. "Tutu, Shaggy come!" she shouted after getting far enough from the road to let them off their leashes. The obedient dogs followed closely behind Anna, only staying a few feet away. Anna decided to take the 3-mile route; this route is her favorite because the small hills wind down past a river.

The morning mist lingered, wrapping itself around the tall blades of grass by the bank. The park was so quiet and peaceful that Anna could hear frogs leaping from the lily pads into the water. This was also Shaggy's favorite route, because he can go swimming, Tutu stays right by Anna's side, watching Shaggy swim. Tutu is way too prissy to get wet. As Anna walked briskly along the bank, she pulled a couple of tennis balls out of her pocket and threw them for Tutu and Shaggy to fetch.

When the threesome came to the top of the hill, Anna saw the plaque nailed to a massive old oak tree. The plaque remarks on the small hole in the tree's trunk, a scar from an old bullet that was once wedged in it. The Historical Society found it in the early 1900s and put the bullet in the city's museum to preserve it. Although Anna had seen the plaque multiple times, she still found it interesting to ponder exactly how the bullet made it into the trunk. Cannon Falls is full of historical surprises. The town is filled with battle scars that continue to tell tales of the events that occurred in 1863.

The morning flew by for Anna, almost quicker than she'd like. Anna hopped out of the shower and checked her phone. One hour to go! The butterflies returned, this time in swarms. Anna wiped the bathroom mirror with her hand. "Suck it up, Anna," she whispered to her reflection as she began applying her makeup before drying her hair and scrunching it into her natural waves.

She double-checked her iPhone's weather app before getting dressed. "Hmm, drizzle with a chance for storms. Peeerrfect." She settled on her choice of wearing her skinny blue jeans, white shirt, black leather jacket, and high-heeled black knee-high boots. *Comfy but cute* she thought to herself while looking at her outfit in the mirror. Checking the time once more, she saw it was 12:45; "Just breathe," she said shakily. Anna made her way downstairs into the kitchen where her mom stood making a salad.

"Oh, honey, you look gorgeous! Great outfit choice. You look adorable," her mom beamed.

"Thanks! Just wish I could stop my heart from pounding like a gong," joked Anna.

"Just think to yourself, 'I'm going to have a good time.' So put your nerves aside and focus on that, and just enjoy the moment." A couple of minutes later, the doorbell rang. Anna and her mom both looked at each other wide-eyed.

"I'll get it!" shouted her dad from his study.

"Oh god," Anna mouthed.

"It's fine. Relax," replied her mom.

"Hi, Mr. Ipswich, nice to meet you. I'm Boston Tate. I'm here to pick up Anna for lunch and a movie." Anna's dad shook Boston's hand and welcomed him into their home.

"Nice to meet you, Boston. Come in. Anna's in the kitchen."

"Hey Boston!" Anna said coolly.

"Hi Anna, Mrs. Ipswich," Boston nodded while extending his arm and shaking her mom's hand.

"Where are you guys going for lunch?" asked her mom.

"Fridays, then we are going to watch the new Halloween movie," replied Boston.

"That'll be fun! Who doesn't love Halloween?" she beamed back.

"Okay... Mom, Dad, we better get going," suggested Anna. As they walked away, Anna's mom let the dogs in the back door. Suddenly a scuffle was heard in the entrance foyer. Anna's mom and dad peered their heads around the corner to see what the commotion was. Boston lay on the floor. Shaggy had jumped up on Boston's back and knocked him completely over. "Oh god, Boston, I am so sorry! Shaggy! Naughty boy!" shouted Anna.

"Are you okay, Boston?" asked her mom with concern. Shaggy sat with his head looking down to the floor and his ears folded down.

"Ha ha... that's okay. Wondered what the heck hit me at first!

Aww... look at him. Shaggy, it's okay. I know you didn't mean it, bud," Boston said while patting the dog on its head. Anna couldn't help but feel warmed by Boston's sweet response. Suddenly, Anna's nerves went away and pure excitement came over her.

"Bye, Shaggy. You ready, Boston? I'm starving." Anna smiled.

"Mustn't keep the lady waiting," Boston joked with Shaggy and then gave Anna that cute little smile she loved so much.

Pearl Jam's "Better Man" played on the stereo in Boston's black 2020 Ford Mustang as the couple drove to lunch. "This car suits you," Anna commented while looking around at the interior.

"Thanks! My parents got it for me for my birthday a couple of years ago. Didn't your parents just get you a car recently? A white Jeep, right?" he asked.

"Yeah, it's a 2017 Latitude."

"It looks really nice, congrats."

"Thanks! So, are you a big Pearl Jam fan?"

"Yes, I love the whole late 90s early 2000s rock music."

"Me too! I like all types of music though," replied Anna.

"So, Brianna said she saw you at Eddie's on Friday night with your friends."

"Oh... yeah... she came over to talk to me for a minute," Anna replied. She could feel herself tensing up at the sound of Brianna's name.

"Yeah, it was weird, because she said that Jay wasn't too friendly though?" Boston asked inquisitively.

"Errr, well she wasn't exactly friendly toward me either. She was actually kind of rude. Jay and Abbey didn't really appreciate it, and neither did I," scoffed Anna.

"Anna, I didn't mean to make you mad," assured Boston. "What did she say to you?"

"I don't really want to get into a 'he said/she said' conversation. I just don't want to make things awkward. I know you're close friends with her, so don't worry about it. It's totally fine."

"Anna, we're not exactly best friends! I know we hang out with the same group of friends, but Brianna likes to make out that we're better friends than what we really are. Besides, we didn't really have a conversation about it, she just texted me on Saturday. I would like to know what she said to you. You can trust me. I won't repeat it to anyone, I promise." Boston said as he grabbed Anna's hand and held it.

His gesture took Anna by surprise, and she couldn't help but smile as she felt a warmth run down her stomach. After running through the whole story with Boston, she felt a lot less anxious about the whole situation. "She can be such a freakin' brat! Ugh... just ignore her, Anna. You have nothing to worry about. She is a lot less important than she thinks she is. The only people who listen to her are those four Brianna wannabes," Boston snorted. Anna smiled, almost feeling triumphant about the whole situation.

After splitting some buffalo wings, Anna and Boston munched down a burger, fries, and a Coke. Then the couple made their way to the movie theater.

"I can't wait to see this movie. I hope it's as good as the original and has some scary scenes that make you jump," laughed Anna.

"Will you hold me if I get scared?" joked Boston as he pouted his lips like a little kid. Once again, he took hold of Anna's hand, and they walked to the concession stand. "You want a drink and some popcorn?" he asked.

"I don't think I could eat a single thing, but I'd never pass up a slushy," replied Anna.

"Agreed. I don't think I could eat either, maybe later. One slushy and a large Dr. Pepper, please," Boston said to the girl working behind the concession counter.

"I'm glad we got here a little early. We should be able to get a good seat," said Anna as they walked through the big red and gold theater doors.

"That's what I was just thinking. I hate getting to a movie late and it's pitch-black when you're trying to find a seat."

Boston sat holding Anna's hand through the movie. A couple of times they giggled when they both jumped during a startling scene. Anna drank in the smell of Boston's cologne, and every time their legs touched or Boston ran his thumb across her hand, Anna felt a little zing of electricity run through her body. During the movie, Anna couldn't help but think to herself, *I wonder if he's going to kiss me?*

"I really enjoyed myself today," Anna said, getting into Boston's car after exiting the movie theater.

"Me too. Listen, Anna, I really like you. I know it's not guy code to admit that on the first date with a girl, but I wanted to tell you that." Anna was shocked. She couldn't believe her ears, but she also felt the exact same way.

"Well, I really like you too, Boston. I've liked you for a while now, if I'm honest," she replied shyly.

"Yeah... I think it's pretty obvious that we've both been flirting with each other for a while now," laughed Boston. "So, what time do you need to be home?"

"I do have some studying to do tonight for that algebra quiz tomorrow. But I could hang out for a little longer if you want to. My mom normally has dinner ready around 6:30. So, as long as I'm home for that, I should be good."

"Cool... so we have about an hour to kill then. Want to go to Starbucks and grab a coffee?"

"Sounds perfect." Anna turned to face the passenger side window as she scrunched up her face and bit her bottom lip, concealing her excitement.

CHAPTER THREE

"Two grande Pumpkin Spice Lattes please," ordered Boston from the barista at the coffee counter. Anna sat looking at a *People Magazine* someone had left behind in the small tan leather chairs in the corner of the coffee shop. "Poor Khloe," said Boston in a snarky tone. Anna frowned as she peered over the top of the glossy magazine to see him standing there laughing at her. "You girls and your celebrity gossip," he joked.

"Whatever!" teased Anna as she leaned forward to take her coffee cup from Boston. Another text message buzzed her phone that was stored inside her purse leaning against her foot. *Those eyes,* she thought to herself as Boston sat staring at her. His big brown almond-shaped eyes looked like they were scanning hers, trying to look straight through them as if he was attempting to read her mind. "So how do you think you will do on the Algebra II quiz tomorrow?" asked Anna.

"Um, okay I think... fingers crossed," Boston said while blowing on his coffee to cool it down.

"What about you?"

"Same. It's starting to get a little harder for me now. I have no idea why I elected to take that class. I have no interest in that stuff anymore," Anna said as she took another sip of her coffee.

"I think you took it because you knew I would be in your class. You're such a little stalker," he teased.

"Errr, okay N-E-R-D!" Anna jested as she gently slapped Boston's hand and shook her head.

"So, I should have asked you this before, but are you dating anyone else?" Boston asked seriously.

Anna replied curiously, "Nope. You?"

"Just a couple of cheerleaders from our school," he replied confidently as Anna sat feeling deflated. "Ha, just joking! You should have seen your face!" exclaimed Boston.

"Whatever, you ass... that wasn't disappointment, that was pure relief." Anna rolled her eyes and laughed.

"Mmmmm... sassy. I like it," Boston hissed as he leaned in closer to Anna. "Can I?" he asked suggestively inches away from her lips.

"Yes," she exhaled slowly. With that, Boston kissed her lips softly in a very gentlemanly yet very sexy way. Anna's stomach did a gigantic loopty loop and bells went off inside her head. Boston pulled back after a couple of seconds.

"You're really beautiful, you know that?" he said rhetorically.

"Thanks. You're not so bad yourself." Once again Anna heard

her phone buzz, announcing yet another text message.

"Jeez, you're popular!" he commented.

"Actually, let me check the time on my phone," Anna said while rumbling around her handbag. She lifted up her iPhone, and three text messages popped up, all from Abbey.

"How's the date going???"

"I hope he's being the gentleman that I know him to be ;)"

"Did you guys kiss yet????" Kissy face emoji, kissy face emoji, kissy face emoji.

Anna shook her head and rolled her eyes, smiling. *If only you knew, girl!!* Anna thought to herself. "It's about twenty till six. We should probably get going," Anna announced.

"Sure thing, let's go," he replied.

After a quick drive home, Boston pulled his car into Anna's driveway. "Even Flow" played quietly in the background. Anna's butterflies once again returned with the anticipation of Boston kissing her again.

"Thanks again, Boston. I had a super fun time with you. I'm really glad you finally asked me out." Anna smiled.

"Me too. The most fun I've had on a date in a while. Do you have plans Wednesday night after school? I have football practice every night till then, but I'd like to hang out with you again."

"No. I don't think so. Maybe we could go to get a bite to eat or a coffee... something like that?" Anna replied.

"'Yes,' she said. 'Something to eat,' she said." Boston smiled as he leaned in closer to Anna. Putting his hands on either side of her face, he kissed her slowly, lightly exploring the inside of her mouth with his tongue. *Mmmm*, Anna thought to herself, *I could get used to this*. They kissed two or three more times before Anna could get herself to get out of his car. Boston walked Anna to her front door.

"Goodnight, Anna," Boston said softly while placing a much more respectable peck on her lips. "See you at school tomorrow!"

"Absolutely. I'll see you then." Anna scrambled to locate the front door key on her key chain with the world spinning around her and her knees feeling weak. Boston headed back to his car as she finally got the key into the lock.

Anna made her way inside the house and into the kitchen where her dad stood cooking. Sundays are spaghetti and salad night. Her mom bakes fresh garlic bread and makes the salad, while her dad makes his so-called 'secret recipe' Bolognese.

"There she is!" exclaimed her dad in a teasing manner.

"How was your date, honey?" asked her mom.

"Wonderful" replied Anna while floating down into one of the kitchen chairs, cheeks burning hot red.

"Oh really! I think I can tell just how well the date went," Anna's mom giggled "He really does seem like a nice boy," her mom said while waving a potholder over the garlic bread, attempting to cool her freshly baked creation. Anna got up from her seat, grabbed some cutlery, and began setting the table. "We'll talk more later," whispered her mom, grinning from ear to ear. Anna could think of nothing else except recollecting the highlights of her date in her head like a SportsCenter play-by-play.

"Boston plays on the football team, right honey?" inquired her dad. Anna shook her head.

"Umm... yeah, that he does."

"Isn't he number 56? I think I remember watching him play in one of the last games that your mom and I attended at the beginning of the season. He's a running back, right? He's very good," Anna's dad nodded his head and continued, "Boston seems like a decent guy from what I can tell. Will we see him around here more often?"

Anna knew exactly what he was getting at. "Yes, Dad, I think you will."

"Good, honey, that's exciting. Your dad will finally have someone at the house he can talk football with," Anna's mom stated while gently shoving her dad in his shoulder.

"Whatever!" her dad joked in a valley girl accent. "He still needs to behave himself and act like a gentleman, though," he added sternly.

After dinner, Anna called Abbey and went through her date in detail with a fine-tooth comb.

"O-M-G!" exclaimed Abbey. "That's freakin' awesome Anna! I

told you he liked you!!"

"Yes! Now, I have to just try and concentrate on studying for that quiz tomorrow. Only God knows how I'm going to do that!" she replied.

Anna stood at her locker, swapping out textbooks for her next class. *Ugh, not good Anna. You should have studied more,* she thought to herself as she slammed the door shut a little harder than usual in frustration. "What's wrong, Anna?" Boston asked as he walked over.

"I'm just mad at myself. I don't think I did so great on that quiz," she replied remorsefully.

"I'm sure you did fine. Don't beat yourself up over it," he assured her.

"How do you think you did?" asked Anna.

"Eh—okay. We'll see, though." He reached down and caught Anna's hand. "Hi, by the way," he smiled, leaning in as Anna gave him a quick peck on the lips. Of course, that turned some heads in the hallways and the whispering set in.

By the time Anna walked out of art class a little over an hour later, everybody was talking about it.

"Jennifer Blake came up to me in drama class and asked if it was true that you and Boston are dating," Abbey smiled, wrinkling her nose.

"Yeah, I knew as soon as we held hands or kissed that the rumor mill would begin a churnin'. It's kind of annoying though," she scoffed. Even though Anna really liked Boston, she had never enjoyed being the center of attention. Anna knew this one aspect of dating THE Boston Tate would be uncomfortable and at times a little irritating.

"Pretty soon you'll be best friends with Brianna and her crew," laughed Jay, playfully poking the bear as he stood next to Abbey while only half paying attention as he played a battleship shooting game on his iPhone.

"Oh yeah! That would be super awesome! LOL... not in a million," she replied firmly.

As school ended for the day, Anna, Abbey, and Jay began to walk down the front steps of the school to head home. A familiar voice from behind grated on Anna's nerves, "Oh Anna, doll!! Boston told me you guys had a good time, and you're seeing each other again on Wednesday. I told Boston that Mark and I will try to meet up with you guys and hang out for a while," Brianna demanded.

Anna turned around begrudgingly and exhaled heavily, "Errr... we'll have to see about that, Brianna. I don't quite know what we're doing yet," replied Anna. *What the hell was he thinking! How did he not get how I felt about her the other day? Did he really agree to us hanging out with the she-devil?!* Anna grimaced.

"Mmm, K! Anyway, gotta run; I have cheerleading practice and all. See ya!" beamed Brianna, pursing her lips as she swiftly turned around and walked back into the school.

"Told you... besties," Jay said with a huge grin on his face, which eventually cracked into a burst of laughter.

"Ugh! I am NOT hanging out with her on Wednesday. It's only our second date, and I have zero desire to spend that time with her. I'd rather spend it getting to know Boston better," Anna said defensively.

"Well, don't get all worked up about it, Anna. I would ask Boston what he said before getting mad at him. You know, innocent until proven guilty," Abbey suggested.

"Yeah, I know you're right. I'll ask him about it later."

"Anyways, let's go home," Jay requested.

Just as Anna pulled up to her house, the rain started to come down heavily. "God, I wish it would just stop raining! It's been raining for four days in a row," Anna said out loud. Fall in Pennsylvania was generally very wet, and Cannon Falls seemed to get more rain than Gettysburg, which is only 40 miles due south of the mountain valley the town sits in. When it rains, it really pours, but the town is as picturesque as they come.

What Anna loved most about the town was the abundance of old Victorian-style homes. Her dream was to one day renovate one of them for her family so her kids could grow up in the area and attend the same schools she did.

Anna was obsessed with interior design and planned to go to a university for architecture and interior design, following in her father's footsteps. Anna's dad has owned his own firm, Ipswich Architecture and Design, for the past 15 years. Although her dad has an office close to the town square, he works remotely from his home office most of the time. He mainly went into the office for meetings with his team or clients, preferring the peace and quiet of home while doing his best design work. The office manager and lead architect, Macy Kay, handled most of the day-to-day operations. Anna's mom worked out of her office three days a week as a counselor for children and families.

Anna has worked about ten hours per week as a paid intern for Ipswich A & D for a little over a year now running errands for the firm, mailing plans to clients out of town, dropping plans off at city hall, and assisting her dad with different tasks when appropriate. Anna's long-term goal was to work for the family firm after graduating college and one day take it over when her dad is ready to retire, but to also keep her interior design passion fed. Anna loves the idea of taking a blank, empty room - a blank canvas - and creating the perfect chic space. Anna wasn't partial to any particular style; she loved ultra-modern, modern farmhouse, contemporary, traditional, etc. For this reason, she tended to rearrange her room and change out the décor often to experiment. Anna also loved the idea of taking an old or dilapidated home and turning it into something beautiful, making the seemingly worthless into something worthwhile.

When Anna pulled up to school the next day, she saw that Boston had parked near her usual spot. "Well, well, well, look who's here," said Jay inquisitively.

"Hmmm... I'm sure he's parking here just to say hi," Anna replied nervously.

"Awww... you're getting butterflies in your tummy, I can tell," teased Abbey, jokingly. "Seriously, though, don't be," she said supportively.

But Anna did feel nervous and excited. Boston walked over as Anna opened her car door. "Hey Anna. Just thought I'd say hi and walk you into school," he smiled.

"Morning!" Anna beamed with a wide grin, pearly whites aglow.

"Hey Jay, what's up?" Boston nodded respectfully.

"Hey Bro, not much. What's up with you? How's practice going?" Jay replied confidently.

Abbey interrupted, "Hey, Boston. Sweet of you to walk Anna into school."

"Yep, I felt like starting my day off right."

"Well, I'll catch up with you later, Anna. Come on Abbey, I'll walk *you* to school," Jay jested, acknowledging Abbey's sign to give the couple some space.

As Jay and Abbey walked off, Boston slipped his hands into Anna's. "What did you do last night, Anna?"

Anna gave his hands an acknowledging squeeze. "Not much. Took the dogs for a walk. Watched my TV shows. Did some homework. Nothing major, really. What did you do after practice?" she replied.

"Oh, I went home and ate myself sick! My mom made BBQ ribs for dinner with baked potato. Her ribs are so freakin' good!"

"Yeah, I can tell you're a bit of a pig," Anna joked.

"Hey! That's not nice. I'm a BIG pig." he snorted with laughter. "So, I was super surprised to hear from Brianna yesterday that you guys had talked about our date on Wednesday. She said that her and Mark might meet up with us?"

"Really? We didn't really discuss it. She made it sound as if you and her had already talked about it. Brianna basically told me that you guys had agreed for them hang with you and me," Anna said in confusion.

"Yeah. No, we didn't. Brianna was rattling on yesterday at lunch, and I basically tuned her out. She's being an idiot. I'll talk to her today about it."

CHAPTER FOUR

Wednesday came quicker than imagined. Anna took longer than usual picking out what outfit to wear because she had her dinner date at Eddie's with Boston straight after school. "Anna. Move it... you're going to be late!" shouted her mom from downstairs in frustration.

"Ugh, whatever. I guess this will have to do," she muttered to herself. Anna had thrown on a pair of black skinny jeans, black knee-high boots, and a white t-shirt with a gray cardigan on top.

"Well don't you look cute... now go! You're making Jay and Abbey late too," her mom ordered while handing Anna her back-pack and giving her a kiss on the cheek. "Call me after school before you go to meet Boston."

"Yeah Mom... I know!" Anna snapped back and instantly regretted sounding like a little brat.

"Anna, watch the attitude," her mom warned.

"I'm sorry, Mom, I didn't mean to be rude. Love you, bye," she said, giving her mom a quick hug.

Anna was disappointed to see that Boston wasn't waiting for her that morning by her parking spot.

"Ugh, I have Physical Ed for my first class today, and I'm not looking forward to it," Jay frowned.

"I didn't realize you disliked it so much?" asked Anna.

"Yeah, Jay, I thought you liked Phys Ed." Abbey chimed in.

"I don't mind it usually, but today were doing square dancing, if you can believe that!" he snorted. "I would rather poke my eye out with a stick than do square dancing!"

"Come on, we know how much you love dancing," teased Abbey.

"Yeah! It's super awesome! It won't be so bad, I guess. I'm partnered up with Chelsea Kent. She's pretty hot," he smiled.

"Well good luck with that!" laughed Anna.

"We better get going to class, Abs," Anna sighed.

Anna couldn't stop the butterflies from returning once again. The anticipation of seeing Boston was getting to her, especially with date night looming. The insecure thoughts popped into her head like text messages... *"What if he's changed his mind? What if Brianna got to him? What if he doesn't want to go out on our date tonight? What if—"*

Suddenly, she felt an instant warm glow inside her stomach as she and Abbey turned the corner in the hallway and could see Boston talking to Justin Holte by Anna's locker. Anna beamed at Boston.

"There she is... running a little behind today, huh?" he joked.

"Just a little," she winked, leaning in and placing a peck on his lips.

"Anna, Abbey, do you girls know Justin?"

Abbey replied quickly, shuffling her shoulder bag. "Yeah, we have Chemistry together," she smiled.

"Hey, Abbey what's up?" Justin asked, tipping his chin up while slinging his backpack over his shoulders.

"Nada. Already waiting for 4 o'clock to roll around. Definitely not in the mood for class today."

"Want to walk to Chemistry together?" he requested.

"Yeah, sure! Just need to get my textbook from my locker." Abbey blushed.

Anna closed her locker door. "Ready? I'll walk you to class," insisted Boston.

"Why, thank you, kind sir," Anna said while taking hold of his hand.

The school bell rang announcing lunch. "Thank God, I'm starving," Anna said to Jay as they walked out of French II class.

"Adieu les etudients, ont un bon apre-midi!" Mrs. Summers called as the students began walking out of class. Mrs. Summers was loved by most of the students at Cannon Falls High who have had the pleasure to have her teach them. She was an attractive woman with dark brown curly hair, which is usually pulled back into a bun. Mrs. Summers liked to hand out French treats, such as chocolate croissants and all sorts of other fun treats to give her students a real taste of France. Although she speaks in French 80% of the time during her class, she is always quick to help her pupils understand. Mrs. Summers is always bubbly but firm which commanded the presence of her class. She was Anna's favorite teacher.

"Merci beaucoup, Madame Summers," Anna called as she exited the classroom door with Jay.

"So did you bring your lunch today or are you buying it here?" asked Jay.

"Buying. I'll probably just get a sandwich and salad. I think Abbey said she was going to meet us downstairs in the cafeteria," replied Anna.

"Mmmm, I could murder a pizza!" Jay exclaimed while digging his wallet out of his back pocket, as they walked down the stairs.

After Anna grabbed her lunch, she headed over to the table where

Abbey sat staring at her phone.

"Hey! How are your classes going today?" asked Anna.

"Fine. Justin was very talkative during Chemistry, more talkative than usual. But I guess we have something in common now, seen as our best friends are dating each other," she grinned.

"Could be," Anna said as Jay sat down.

"Looking forward to your date, Anna?" asked Abbey.

"Totally! Just wish it would hurry up and get here," she replied excitedly.

"Looks like you won't have to wait too long to see Boston again, or should I say your new man? He's coming over," Abbey nodded, widening her eyes at Anna with a grin.

"Hey guys, do you mind if I sit with you?" Boston asked as he took a seat.

"Of course not. Sit down, man," replied Jay. "Where are you guys going tonight?" he continued.

"Eddie's... right, Anna?" he double-checked with Anna.

"Yep, Eddie's," she confirmed. Anna felt excited that Boston decided to come and sit with her and her friends instead of with Brianna and his usual group of friends.

As she looked up, she could feel someone watching her, and, sure enough, she turned to see Brianna glaring at her. *If looks could kill*, she thought to herself. Clearly, Brianna was not happy that her circle of friends, who had been mostly impenetrable for the last couple of years, was beginning to crack.

Anna couldn't help but feel a little justified, and, feeling brazen, decided to give Brianna a little smile and nod. Brianna sharply turned her head away to face one of her 'wannabes' as she rolled her eyes. *Ha! Your little tricks aren't working this time, little miss thing,* Anna thought to herself.

Four o'clock finally hit. Anna cleaned off her desk quicker than ever, throwing everything into her backpack while buzzing with excitement. "Guys, come on," Anna pushed as Abbey and Jay came to meet her by the school's front door. Abbey and Jay just snickered at Anna's assertive behavior. They were well aware of her anxiousness to get to the diner to meet Boston. Anna drove a little faster than usual to drop Jay and Abbey off at their houses.

"Have fun, Anna. Don't do anything we wouldn't do!" shouted Jay as he walked away from her car and toward his Cape Cod-style home with gray wooden shingles and white shutters.

"Ha... ha... Jay, you're sooo original," she laughed back.

"Do you want to freshen up your makeup at my house?" quizzed Abbey.

"Sure, I'll just put some on in your driveway," replied Anna. "I just want to get there so he isn't waiting too long for me at Eddie's," she added.

"Cool! I have to say, I think Justin seems like a super nice guy and obviously gorgeous. I think you should find out if he's dating anyone. Like, I know he was dating Katie Hoffman, but I'm pretty sure she broke up with him to date Tre Wilks," Abbey smiled, raising her eyebrows.

"OK. Yeah, I will for sure say something to Boston. I'll find a way to slide it into the conversation so it doesn't sound obvious."

"Sweet!" Abbey exclaimed.

"Jeez, Abbey, this is the most excited I've seen you get about a guy in a long time. You're going to make Alex jealous!" Anna said while applying her light blue eye shadow.

"Ugh! Whatever, Anna. We're just friends and nothing else. Anyway, like I've said before, I wouldn't want to date him. It could ruin our friendship if it didn't work out. We just like to flirt with each other for fun. Alex feels the same way," she replied, beginning to sound testy.

"I was just joking, Abs. I didn't mean to annoy you," laughed Anna. "I'll call you tonight after I get home and give you the scoop about Justin."

CHAPTER FIVE

Anna pulled up to Eddie's Diner just in time for the light misty rain to begin falling. The diner was quiet which was perfect for their date. As she walked up to the glass double doors, Anna could see Boston talking on the phone. *God, you look H-O-T!* Anna screamed excitedly in her head. She couldn't help but feel a rosy shade of blush burn across her cheeks and a grin spread across her mouth.

"I mean it dude! You just need to keep her away tonight... you're the one driving. Just make an excuse as to why you can't come here. Tell her whatever you want to. I don't want her here, bro, regardless of what she says." With that, Boston hung up his phone and put it back into his jacket pocket. "Sorry," he said, as Anna approached the booth.

"No... don't be. What was that all about?" asked Anna, confused. Suddenly a bad feeling came over her. She already knew his answer.

"That was Mark. He told me that Brianna told/ordered him to stop by here tonight to say *hi* to us," Boston scoffed.

Anna felt her stomach sink "Oh?!"

"Sorry, Anna. She's such a brattish control freak. Anyways, I told him to not come here. We can leave and find somewhere else to eat if you'd prefer?" he offered.

"No, that's silly. It will be fine. It sounds like Mark knows not to bring her here. Besides, I'm totally craving a cheeseburger and shake!" Anna smiled.

"Ha! Me too," he beamed. "You look really pretty by the way. I like your hair like that," Boston said as he leaned over the table and planted a soft, elongated kiss on her lips.

I'm so glad I decided to do a side braid, Anna thought as she smiled.

"Thanks. You look great too!" she replied.

"Wow, I'm starving! I can't decide what to eat. Everything sounds good to me right now," Boston said while flipping the menu over to the view items on the back.

As the couple sat eating their dinner, the rain began to come down harder outside. The mist had turned into a complete and utter downpour. Thunder began to roll and shake the diner's windows. "Jeez!" Anna jumped when a bright flash of fork lightning hit, followed quickly by a loud crack of thunder.

"Ha! You okay over there?" jested Boston.

"That was super loud!" Anna laughed at herself.

"I know. That lightning was crazy bright," he added.

"It's so freakin' dark outside. You can't even tell it's sunset."

"If you're scared, I can come sit by you," Boston pouted.

"I think I'll be fine," Anna squinted her eyes back at him for making fun of her and smiled. Anna noticed a truck pulling up with its headlights on bright. *They're going to get drenched getting out in this*, she thought to herself.

The driver got out of the truck with an umbrella, scampered around to the passenger side, and opened the door. "What the hell?" questioned Boston.

"What?" replied Anna. She kept watching as a blonde stepped out of the truck and huddled under the umbrella. The unfortunate holder of the umbrella, now barely covered, was getting soaked by the rain.

"Anna, you might want to finish your food a little quicker so we can get our check. We can get dessert or coffee from somewhere else," Boston suggested while gritting his teeth.

"What's the rush?" she replied, confused.

"That's Brianna and Mark. I told him not to bring her here and he choked, following her orders anyway. That freakin' wuss!" Anna had never seen Boston so annoyed before except maybe when a ref made a bad call out on the field.

"Boston, honestly, it's okay. We'll deal with it. Sure, she's irritating, but I can handle my own with Little Miss Priss," Anna said, placing her hand on his forearm.

"I know you can. I just don't want her to ruin our date," he said, taking her hand in his.

"She won't... it'll be fine. Just relax," she replied reassuringly.

Just then, Brianna burst through the doors in jeans that would require pliers to remove them. "Oh... oh my god! Yuck!" she announced loud enough for the entire diner to hear.

She is such a freakin' attention-seeker, Anna thought to herself.

Brianna looked around and spotted Boston and Anna. Boston got up from his side of the booth and went over to sit next to Anna. "Oh, hi guys! What a coincidence! I really thought you would be gone by now," said Brianna, walking over to the booth.

"Yeah... okay, Brianna," Boston scoffed.

Brianna completely ignored Boston. "So, it's okay if we sit with you guys for a couple of minutes, right?" she said, planting herself down before they had a chance to answer. Mark walked up with his eyes on the floor.

"Hey guys," he smiled without making eye contact, acting like a dog with its tail between its legs.

"Hey Mark. I guess you didn't do what I asked you to do earlier then," Boston said sarcastically.

"I tried man, sorry," he replied and shrugged his shoulders.

"What are you guys talking about?!" snapped Brianna.

"Oh... nothing Bree. No worries," Mark replied, putting his arm around her.

"So, how's it going, Anna? I see you guys have already eaten. I so wish I could eat like that," Brianna said cattishly.

"Great. I work out five times a week. I love food. I basically work out to eat," Anna replied confidently.

"Nothing worse than taking a girl out on a date and all she eats is a salad. Totally annoying," added Boston as he held Anna's hand.

"Well, what are you guys doing after this? I heard it's supposed to stop storming soon. I think they said the severe thunderstorm watch would be over by seven o'clock," said Brianna.

"Not sure yet, maybe Starbucks," replied Boston.

"Ah dude, I love Starbucks. Its sooo good. I love those frozen slushy things," Mark chimed in. Anna didn't mind Mark. He's not the sharpest tool in the shed, but a good football player, relatively harmless and a pretty friendly guy to everyone.

"What are you two doing after you stop bugging us?" asked Boston boldly.

"We were supposed to go to Mary Mack's house, but Syreena just canceled on me. Apparently, she and Braidon got into a massive fight so she's not going out now. I swear those two are the biggest drama queens of all time," Brianna scoffed while checking her phone again in the hopes that Syreena had changed her mind. "Ugh, guess she really isn't going. That totally sucks!"

"What were you guys going to do at Mary Mack's house anyway?" asked Anna as she rolled her eyes.

"Oh, come on! You know what we were going to do. It's the only reason why anyone would be going there. Apparently, Caroline Roads, Rebecca Long, and the boys went there last Saturday night and did the rhyme thing, and they got totally freaked out! They said they couldn't drive away fast enough. Becky said they nearly hit a car on their way home, because they freaked out so bad. Ha ha!" she laughed.

"Wait a minute, last Saturday night? Was it on 106 where they nearly hit someone?" inquired Anna.

"Um, yeah, I think so. Why?" she replied.

"Because it was my car that they nearly hit! They were driving like drunken lunatics, and they came super close to hitting me and my friends head-on!" Anna said as she grabbed her phone to text Abbey. "Alex Preston was in the back of my car and couldn't really tell who it was, but it must have been them. Well, this solves that little mystery. So, they were driving like crazy people because they had seen Mary's ghost?!" exclaimed Anna.

"Yes, they did. Caroline swore on her life that they saw her right after they finished reciting the first verse. Can you imagine how freaky that would be?!" Brianna's voice broke in excitement. "Anyway, we were supposed to go and check it out tonight with Syreena and Braidon. I want to see for myself. Wouldn't you, Anna?" asked Brianna.

"No. Not really. I think it's all just a stupid legend that way too many people get caught up in. I have zero desire to go there!" she replied.

"Ugh! Whatever. I think you are just s-c-a-r-e-d and you don't want to admit it."

"Brianna, get over yourself! Give it a rest, you sound like you're ten years old," Boston snarled.

"Wait. I forgot. What's the deal with the old house again and this Mary Mack lady?" inquired Mark.

"Seriously, Mark, you are so stupid! How many times do I have to repeat this to you?!" Brianna hissed.

"I'll tell you, Mark," Anna chimed in. "Do you remember the old rhyme 'Miss Mary Mack, Mack, Mack. All dressed in black, black, black'?"

"Yeah," he replied.

"Okay, well there is a true story behind the children's rhyme."

Boston interrupted her, "Anna, are you sure you don't want to head to Starbucks now?"

"No, Boston, it's okay. I'll tell Mark the story, and I think the four of us should head to Mack's house," Anna said, firmly wanting to prove that she wasn't afraid. There was no way she would let Brianna reap the benefits of thinking that she had one over on her.

"Are you sure?" Boston said, amazed at what Anna just announced.

"Yep!" Anna replied confidently. "Sound okay to you, Brianna?" Anna challenged.

"Sounds like a plan to me," she clapped back with a stone-faced expression.

"Anyway. So, Mark, have you heard the full rhyme in Cannon

Falls?"

"Umm... yeah, but I can't remember what it is," he replied.

"The rhyme that we know has been drastically changed over the course of 200 years. The original rhyme is based on Mary Mack, a bride-to-be who lived in the house off of 106. Today it's owned by the park, but kids sneak into the house all the time due to the legend that surrounds the place. The original rhyme was believed to have been created by a group of young girls in Cannon Falls around 1837."

Brianna interrupted, "Yes, it goes, *'Miss Mary Mack, Mack, Mack. All dressed in black, black, black. With silver buttons, buttons, buttons. All down her back, back, back. She lost her groom, groom, groom. Therefore, she'll roam, roam, roam. Till yellow ribbons, ribbons, ribbons. Bring him back home, home, home,"* she sang.

"Right," Anna said, taking the reins of the discussion once again.

"Why did the girls make up the rhyme about her?" asked Mark.

"Because her fiancé, Officer Benjamin Watts, went off to battle near Gettysburg and never came back. No one knows what happened to him. They were supposed to get married when he returned. She stayed at the house waiting for him, hoping he would one day return. They say she died of a broken heart. Mary and Benjamin had been together since they were children. He was four years older than her.

Mary lived to an old age, but as the years went by, the townspeople began to make up stories about her and her hermit lifestyle. She stayed to herself and always wore a black dress. After her parents died, she only came out of her house to get necessities but didn't speak to anyone. Mary basically just gave up on life, and I guess she didn't want to live it without him. She refused to move on and try to be happy," she finished.

"Wow, that's a pretty sad story," Mark commented while scratching his head.

"Yeah, people said they would just see her roaming by the windows inside her house, looking out for him. She continued to tie yellow ribbons on the tree branches outside of her house for decades, hoping they would welcome him home one day, hence the rhyme," Anna added.

"What does the ghost story have to do with this story?" asked Mark.

"Because it's an old story or legend, if you will, that if you go to her house, sit down, and say the rhyme with the clapping, her ghost will appear before you finish it. God, don't you listen!? We just spoke about this five minutes ago when we talked about Caroline and Becky," snapped Brianna.

"Brianna! Calm down, babe! Just relax. I'm tired of your nagging," Mark finally stood up for himself.

"Oh... um... sorry, honey. I'll make it up to you later," she replied while pecking him on the lips multiple times and holding his face in her hands. It was the first time Anna saw Brianna back down to someone. She obviously knew she had gone too far. There's no way she would jeopardize her relationship with the football team's quarterback.

"That's okay, babe," Mark replied while a grin crept across his face, and he kissed the back of her hand. Finally, the thunderstorm had ended, and the rain had stopped.

"Anna, do you want to go get Starbucks?" asked Boston as he signed the back of the diner's check.

"Thanks for coming in guys!" announced the waiter.

"I wouldn't mind stopping by on the way to Mack's house," she replied.

"Okay, let's get going then," Boston grabbed her and pulled her out of the booth.

"We'll meet you guys there in 30 minutes?" asked Brianna.

"Yeah, see you there," Anna replied.

With that, Anna and Boston left Eddie's and headed for their cars. "I'll see you at Starbucks, then we can drop your car off at your house on the way to the Mack House?" Boston shouted from his car that was parked a few spaces away from Anna's.

"Yep, I'll see you in a bit," Anna shouted back. Anna got into her car and suddenly had a strange feeling come over her. *What if she really is still haunting the old place?* she pondered.

Anna didn't remember ever seeing a ghost before, apart from the goofy fake ones at Halloween. For some reason, she just had no desire to pursue the paranormal. Anna couldn't help but feel a little nervous about it. *Don't be such a wimp, Anna!* she told herself firmly.

CHAPTER SIX

A couple of minutes later, Anna arrived at Starbucks feeling satisfied with the fact that she had beaten Boston there. Anna rushed inside to get out of the dark, chilly fall night and headed straight for the counter. Ordering two caramel macchiatos, Anna thought back to her first date with Boston less than a week earlier. "We'll call your name when your order is ready," advised the blonde barista with a nose ring and long, thick dreads.

At the corner of the café were four soft wingback chairs by a coffee table. *That'll do*, Anna thought to herself, and she headed over to the area. As she sat her purse down on the chair, Anna heard the male barista from behind the counter call her name. Just then, she heard the bell from the above the door ding; it was Boston.

"Hey! Good timing, our drinks are ready," Anna greeted him.

"Oh sweet! You stay there, I'll go get them," he said, walking over to the counter. "Thanks for the coffee!" Boston beamed as he sat the drinks down on the table.

"No problem. This has been the first chance I've had to pay for something on our date," Anna smiled back.

"Sooo..." Boston said while taking off his jacket, "Are you sure you really want to go to Mary Mack's house? I really don't want you to feel pressured into doing something just 'cause Brianna's being catty," he said with concern.

"No, honestly, it's okay. I want to go now," Anna insisted.

"Okay, as long as you're good, I'm cool with that," Boston said while squeezing her knee. "So, have you ever been in the old place?"

"No. I know they open it up on special occasions at the park, but I've never been inside. Have you?" she replied.

"Yeah, just with my parents. Smells like an old musty fire pit. It's not in the best shape; just some old wooden tables and chairs, a few old brass candlesticks sitting about the place - you know - general stuff like that. The fireplace is huge, though, for the size of the place. I mean, it's just a little house! They also have one of her black mourning dresses on display in the bedroom; it's supposed to be one of the dresses she wore."

"I heard she never wore another color of dress again once it was obvious that Benjamin Watts wasn't coming home and was presumed dead. I guess she just never stopped mourning the loss of him," replied Anna. Anna felt for the first time in her life a glimpse of what Mary went through. Anna had only been out on two dates with Boston, but she already knew that her feelings for him were way stronger than anything she had felt before. *I feel like I could fall in love with him*, she thought suddenly to herself. Anna shook her head. *Calm down, Anna. You're getting way too carried away!* her subconscious added.

"In a way, I don't know if it's right to go there and mess with this type of thing, you know? Like we're being disrespectful or something?" Anna questioned.

"I see where you're coming from. So, let's just not go," Boston replied.

"But... let's just do it this once to shut Brianna up. I think the old story is a bunch of mumbo jumbo anyway," Anna snorted.

After Anna and Boston finished their coffees, they headed to Anna's house to drop off her car. As Anna pulled her car up into her driveway, she noticed that it was already 7:30. Because her curfew is 9 o'clock during the week, Anna made a point to let Boston know when she got in his car that they couldn't stay too long. "We should have plenty of time to meet up with Brianna and get you home on time. Trust me, I'm not looking to get on your parents' bad side," he replied with a cheeky smile.

"Lord, it's getting windy again outside," Anna pointed out as she could see the dried leaves circling their way around like a small tornado on the damp pavement in front of Boston's headlights. Is it supposed to storm anymore?" asked Anna. She could feel her nerves getting the best of her. Even though she didn't fully believe in the legend, the very idea of it was still a little spooky. Just being in that old house at night is creepy enough in its own right.

"I don't think so, but I'm not sure. If you're changing your mind, I can always text Brianna and make up some excuse as to why we can't meet them. Just let me know before we get too close to the house?" Boston questioned.

He could feel her hand getting a little clammy and noticed that Anna was shaking her leg. "I appreciate it... but I won't though," Anna replied with determination.

"Alright," he said while giving her hand a soft squeeze. "You're the boss!" he chuckled.

When they pulled up at the Mack House, Brianna and Mark were already in the driveway. "Seems like Brianna is the eager beaver tonight," commented Boston. "Typically, she's the fashionably late type of girl, as you can imagine," he laughed.

"Umm, hmm," Anna retorted.

The old home sat quiet and dark; no lights lit the parking lot, just the one lonely streetlamp from the main road stretching its glow across to the Mack House. Water droplets trickled down the dark gray wooden shingles. Two small windows faced the main road, and two dormer windows were perched on the roof above.

The dark thick glass of the windows reflected Mark's headlights. The windowsills had paint chipping away from the wood.

The dormer windows on the roof looked in worse shape than the windows on the main floor. The weathered roof was flanked by two brick chimneys. On top of the vaulted roof sat a small, black, rusty weathervane, pointing west. The weathervane had a cross perched on top of its N, E, S, W letters. Both sides of the house had light-shaded brick that was covered in ivy. It appeared to have over one hundred vines of ivy webbed across the brick, looking like it had been there almost as long as the house itself. At the back of the house, large trees lined the perimeter like a giant green wall.

Anna got out of the car and walked around to the back of the house; Boston followed her. As she approached one of the small windows, she tried to see through into the house, barely making out what appeared to be a small four-poster bed in a room. "Wow, these people really didn't allow much light to flow into their houses," she mumbled.

"No kidding. Come on, let's get inside before the bottom of your pant legs get soaked," he said, pointing down to the long blades of muddy, wet grass.

"Why then, if you were a true gentleman, you would carry a lady through this soggy landscape," joked Anna.

"Ha! Here, jump on my back!"

"Okay!" she giggled while he gave her a piggyback ride around to the front door.

"So just exactly how are we supposed to get in the old place?" asked Boston as he approached Brianna and Mark.

"Well, let's just say that J Duncan told me a little secret," replied Brianna. She then bent down and reached under the steps in front of the door. Her hand felt around in a dark hole before she pulled out a small rubber black box that contained a key.

"Jeez... the Historical Society doesn't know about that?! I mean, how long has it been there?" asked Anna in shock.

"Years, apparently, but people have to swear to secrecy that they won't tell anyone!" Brianna said while squinting her eyes at Anna.

"I'm not going to say anything," snarled Anna. "Besides, people have been sneaking into this place for years... one way or another."

"Yeah, true," replied Mark.

"Let's just get on with it," smiled Brianna, giddy with excitement. Anna took a deep breath. Boston took hold of her hand and squeezed it gently as she looked over at him. Boston shot back his award-winning gorgeous smile making her feel reassured. Brianna unlocked the door and gave it a little jiggle, but it wouldn't open.

"Watch out," said Mark. With that, he gave the black door a firm push causing it to pop open.

"The wood probably became a little warped from all the damp weather over the years." Mark's dad runs his own carpentry business in town and Mark helps him on weekend jobs when he doesn't have a football game or practice. As soon as the two couples walked in through the open door, the smell of the large, smoky old fireplace hit them hard.

CHAPTER SEVEN

The group turned on their lanterns and flashlights.

"Ugh... it smells like ten bonfires in here!" complained Brianna.

"It does smell very smoky in here, I'll give you that," replied Boston.

"Yeah. Pretty much what I expected," added Anna. "These old places all smell. Considering the fireplace was the sole source of warmth and used for cooking, they were basically running 24x7, especially during the colder seasons."

"Ugh, god, why is it so dirty in here? Look at that cobweb; it's H-U-G-E! I mean doesn't the Historical Society clean this place?" Brianna said as she shined her flashlight into the corner of the ceiling near the window. Thoroughly grossed out, she shook her body in disgust. "Let's make this quick. I already feel like I need a shower."

"Agreed, I need to get home soon anyway," replied Anna.

"So, what are we supposed to do, exactly?" Boston said as he looked at the small oval picture frame hanging by the fireplace. "Is this Watts?" he asked.

"Let me see. I saw a picture of him once in a history class a few years ago," replied Anna as she leaned in to take a closer look at the picture. "Yeah, I'm pretty sure that's Benjamin."

"Hmm, he's kinda hot!" Brianna retorted in surprise as she walked up to look at the picture.

Benjamin was wearing his Union military uniform. The picture was black and white, but you could see the different light and dark tones in the layered, wavy hair that came down to his cheekbones in a short-to-medium-length style. His sideburns framed his attractive face and strong jawline. Anna could almost feel his light blue eyes staring into her. He was the epitome of the young, distinguished, very handsome Civil War soldier that Hollywood liked to portray in its movies.

"If his heart matches his exterior, it's no wonder Mary fell completely in love with him," Anna said out loud to herself. "So tragic that he never came home."

Seeing Benjamin's picture made the story feel more real to Anna. It wasn't just a legend or story that she had heard growing up in Cannon Falls. These people were real, with real lives and real emotions. "This almost feels disrespectful to be here now, like we're playing with these people's lives and hearts for entertainment," Anna said to Boston while taking his pinky finger in her hand and looking down to the floor like a child that had just been scolded.

"We can still leave, Anna." Boston replied.

"Anna, come on!!" exclaimed Brianna, sensing that Anna was beginning to change her mind. Brianna didn't like the idea of her paranormal investigation being a wash. "Unless this is too scary for a sweet girl like you?" she continued in a sarcastic, derogatory tone.

"No. Let's just do this stupid thing and get the heck out of here," Anna snapped back, knowing she would never hear the end of it if she backed out now. *Yes, Anna you have succumbed to peer pressure, you complete weak ass,* her subconscious yelled to herself.

Brianna threw a little wooly blanket on the cold, dusty floorboards and placed a small lantern in the middle. She gestured for Anna to sit on the opposite side, facing her. Boston and Mark just stood watching the girls. "Ready?" asked Brianna.

"Sure!" replied Anna sarcastically.

"Okay, here we go! *Miss Mary Mack, Mack, Mack. All dressed in black, black, black...*" The girls clapped their hands in time with the rhyme, following the centuries-old, choreographed clapping sequence.

"*With silver buttons, buttons, buttons. All down her back, back, back...*" The girls continued with the rhyme as they looked at each other and around the room, searching for a sign of any movement. But there was no motion. Everything was still.

They continued with the second verse, *"She lost her groom, groom, groom. Therefore, she'll roam, roam, roam. Till yellow ribbons, ribbons, ribbons. Bring him back home, home, home."* Anna paused as her eyes darted around the room again. The atmosphere was changing, and she could feel it happening. A cool breeze circulated from left to right, getting colder - so cold that Anna's lips began to tremble.

"Do you guys feel that?" asked Brianna as her eyes widened like a deer in the headlights. She crossed her arms and rubbed her shoulders briskly, attempting to warm herself up.

"Feels like someone has a deep freezer door open," replied Boston. Even he was beginning to look weirded out.

"Mark, I want to leave. This is freaking me out," Brianna said scared. The cold breeze began to calm down, but the house was still freezing cold. Faint footsteps could be heard coming suddenly from the bedroom. Anna just sat frozen in panic, her face completely still and unable to move.

"Dude, what the hell is going on?!" exclaimed Mark.

"Shh... stop talking," ordered Anna whispering. Suddenly, the lantern between Anna and Brianna blew out.

"Arghh!" screamed Brianna. Boston's flashlight went out, flickered on, then off, then on, and finally off again. Mark was holding the only light in the house. Brianna was now completely frozen with fear.

"Dude! I'm getting the hell out of here!" shouted Mark.

Just then his flashlight went out. The only dim light in the house came from the streetlamp outside on the main, illuminating the room. Mark jumped back. The foursome around the room at each other not knowing what to do. wanted to run to the front door, but a mixture of fascination and sheer terror held them still.

"Do you hear that?" asked Anna.

"Hear what?" replied Boston. The gentle breeze began to flow through the room once again. "What... what is that? What the—" Anna strained to listen, trying to make some sense of what she was hearing.

"Holy shh—" Boston jumped back from the window over to where Mark was standing on the other side of the room. The girls quickly jumped up and ran over to them.

Anna turned her head sharply toward the dimly lit window. She gasped as a black, shadowy figure came toward them. The figure got closer and closer to them until they could see the outline of a big dress. The figure continued to move slowly closer and closer. Anna could smell an overpowering scent of flowery lavender perfume filling in the air. Suddenly, Anna could hear a woman whimpering and sobbing. The soft crying faded in and out – audible for a second and then gone like a bad Bluetooth connection or a light switch being flipped on and off.

"Anna, come on, we're getting the hell out of here!" Boston said as he grabbed her hand and pulled her toward the front door.

Anna could barely move her legs. "Wait, wait! I can hear it again. It's clearer now," she said, tilting her head to one side as she

road, gently
looked
They

hear her! Do you guys hear that?!" she

in and out but a little louder this time.
:ould not make heads or tails of what
moment, the voice shouted clearly,

"Come on, Anna, we're leaving... now!" Boston shouted to Anna and the four of them ran out the front door and back to their cars. Nobody said a word. They just all got in their cars. Anna and Boston watched Mark quickly run back and lock the front door shakily before he bent down to place the key back in its secret spot.

Still in the parking lot of the Mack House, Anna and Boston sat silently inside Boston's car in total disbelief of what they had just witnessed. "Anna... Anna, I'm so sorry, I should never have let you go there. Stupid Brianna! Are you okay?" he said turning her to face him. Anna tried to shake the wealth of emotions running through her, but the fear and sadness were overwhelming.

"Err, yeah, I guess," she replied as tears filled her eyes. "Can you drive please? I just want to get away from here, fast."

"Of course. I'm so sorry, Anna. I really am," Boston said respectfully. He revved up the engine and turned on the stereo. Pearl Jam's "Jeremy" played in the background. Boston felt guilty. It was only their second date. He shouldn't have let Anna be put in that position. He should have told Brianna to piss off, he thought, shaking his head from left to right. It was supposed to be a nice quiet night together - hopefully, a prequel to a third date - nothing like what they had just gone through. "I hope I didn't mess things up for us, Anna. Some of the people who run in my circle really aren't such nice people. I honest to God didn't want her around us tonight. I didn't expect it to turn out this way. I understand if this has left a sour taste in your mouth and if you're mad at me," he said sorrowfully.

Wait a minute, what is he saying?! Anna thought to herself. She had been daydreaming about what just happened and far away in her own head. His words brought her sharply back to reality.

"What are you talking about, Boston? I'm not mad at you. I'm mad at myself!" Anna insisted as she leaned over and kissed him on the cheek.

"Anna, I know this isn't the right time to discuss our relationship, but whatever just happened really freaked me out, and all I wanted to do was just protect you. I've never felt so protective over another person like that before," Boston said anxiously.

"Have you ever encountered anything like that before?" Anna interrupted.

"Never, but it made me realize just how strongly I feel for you. I'm serious, Anna. I've never felt like this before. I want you, Anna, you and no one else, and I don't want anyone else to have you either. Will you be my girlfriend... be exclusive or whatever you want to call it?" Boston chuckled at himself feeling like a complete cheese ball.

Anna's stomach exploded with butterflies and did flip-flops all at once. "Of course, I don't want anybody else either, Boston." With that, Boston pulled to the side of the road in her subdivision and kissed Anna deeply, holding her face in his hands as she dragged her fingers through his hair. "God, I love kissing you," Anna whispered heavily.

As they pulled into her driveway, Anna's thoughts returned once again to what had just happened at the Mack House. She had never experienced anything like that before and felt thoroughly weirded out by the whole turn of events. It felt like a nightmare or like she had just awoken from some really strange dream. The whole thing was surreal.

"Boston, I need you to be honest with me. Did you hear anything back at the house? Well, obviously, other than Brianna's cries?"

"No. I just saw the figure. I'm guessing it was her figure," he replied.

"But nothing else?" she requested.

"No, just Brianna and Mark. That's all. Why? What did you hear?" Boston's interest spiked as he began to wonder what Anna was referring to.

"Oh, I don't know. I thought I heard something, but my head was spinning at the time. I was having a serious panic attack," she snorted.

"Well, tell me! What did you think you heard? It's just between me and you. You can tell me, Anna," he added.

"Okay, but don't think I'm crazy."

"I won't—shoot," he smiled.

"Well, before we saw 'her' at the window, when Brianna and I were still sitting on the floor, I thought I heard a woman sobbing. But it was really faint, and it kept fading in and out."

Boston raised his eyebrows, "Really?"

"Yes, but then when she appeared at the window, I heard it again. Only this time it was louder and... and I could hear whispering, but I couldn't make out what she was saying. It was a mixture of whispering and crying."

"Holy shit!" commented Boston.

"The crying and whispering were like... how can I put this... Hmm. Okay, it was like when you have bad reception on your cell phone. Like when you have a bad signal and when you are trying to talk to someone but the sound keeps cutting in and out, so you only hear pieces of what the person's trying to say. Does that make sense?" she asked.

"Yeah, total sense. So, you heard her crying and maybe whispering something to you?"

"Yeah. I think it was her. Who else could it have been? I couldn't understand the whispers apart from one word right before you grabbed me, and we ran out of the house."

"Well... what did you hear?" he said, intrigued.

"It was just one word, clear as day - 'help'" she replied, shaking her head once again in disbelief. "I have the sneaking suspicion that she was talking about Watts. In fact, I would say I'm 100% sure that's who she was referring to."

"Jeez... that's crazy!."

"I know right! I can't believe it either. Did you also smell the flowery perfume when she appeared? It was sooo strong," asked Anna.

"No, not at all. Just that same smoky, moldy smell. Huh—strange."

"Wow! Weird! I wonder if Brianna heard or smelled anything?"

"I don't know. I'm going to ask Mark tomorrow, see if she said anything. Although I'm sure Brianna will be full of gossip tomorrow at school, and I'm sure she'll be talking to us in the morning about it. Brianna knows this will pull a lot of attention once word gets out," Boston rolled his eyes.

"Maybe. Maybe we don't tell her about the crying or whispering unless she brings it up. I don't want Brianna making a mockery of it more than she already will be," Anna said as she tapped her fingers on her teeth and stared at Boston.

"Of course, whatever you think is best."

"Well, I should probably get inside. I'm already 20 minutes late. Thanks for dinner, and believe it or not, I had a great time with my *boyfriend*," Anna jested.

"I see how it is. Now you're going to mock me. You're mean," exclaimed Boston playfully.

"You know I'm just teasing, come here," she said while leaning over and kissing him.

"Now that's the nice girl I know," smiled Boston.

"Ha! Goodnight," Anna said while pushing open the passenger side door.

"No, no... not so fast. I'll get that," Boston shouted as he quickly sprang out of his seat and in a flash was by her side of the car, opening the door for her.

"You're so silly... but I do appreciate your chivalry, sir," Anna jested once again.

"Hey, it's our early days still... and remember, I am a gentleman," he beamed back. "Goodnight, Anna. I'll see you in the parking lot at school tomorrow," Boston said, planting a quick peck on her lips before she ran into her house. Boston took a deep, long breath as he watched her go inside. *Hmm... I'm in freakin' trouble with this one,* he thought to himself. *She's amazing.*

CHAPTER EIGHT

"Mom! I've got to talk to you!" Anna demanded as she waltzed into the living room like a gust of wind. Her mom was laying on the couch, watching *Wives of New England*.

"Oh, hi darling! How was your date with Boston? Did you have a good time? You're missing *Wives* which means someone is a little late," she added in an inquisitive tone.

"I know I'm late... I'm really sorry. But, technically, I was home on time, just not in the house." Anna smirked.

"Oh really? And what were you doing in the driveway, miss?" she said with raised eyebrows.

"We were just talking about what happened earlier tonight, and yes, I had a great time," replied Anna.

"Ha ha... just giving you a hard time, honey. What is it that you wanted to talk to me about?"

"Have you been to the Mack House before?"

"Yes, I have. Why? Where are you going with this?" her mom said as she paused the television and sat up. "Come, sit down," she patted the couch beside her.

"Okay, just don't say anything till I'm finished."

"Fine, my lips are sealed," she said while pretending to lock her lips and throw away the key.

"So did you happen to go at night?"

"Don't tell anyone, Anna, or you're grounded for life! But yes, I went there at night with some friends when I was in high school. We thought it would be fun to find out if the legend was true."

"Did anything strange happen?" asked Anna intrigued.

"No, not really. It just got a little cold. We figured it was just an old house that was drafty. But that was it... wait, why?"

"Well don't freak out, but we went there tonight with Brianna and Mark."

"Anna! You shouldn't be going there at night. That place isn't safe; it's falling apart! Regardless of what the Historical Society claims, it's not being taken care of like it used to be. Wait... how did you get in there?" exclaimed her mom.

"Ummm, that's not important."

"Anna! Don't tell me you guys broke in or something stupid like that."

"Mom... chill. Jeez, of course we didn't break in. Let's just say we walked in through the front door, and I can't tell you anymore," Anna insisted.

Anna's mom knew that Anna was a good girl who was very

responsible, so she dropped this line of questioning. "Go on... continue your story then. But before you do, let me say this - Don't do it again, Anna, and I mean it!" demanded her mom.

"I won't. I promise. Anyway, something really freaky happened, Mom. We saw her, and she spoke to me..." Anna continued to tell her mom the details of the encounter.

After Anna finished recounting her story, her mom wasn't sure what to say. She knew by Anna's face that she wasn't joking or lying; she was 100% serious. "Well, honey, are you sure that smell wasn't Brianna's perfume? Maybe the whispers were just your imagination working overtime, given what you all saw? I believe that you all believe you did see Mary or someone/something, but I'm firstly trying to figure out if there is a rational explanation."

"I don't think Brianna was wearing flowery perfume. It was so strong that I would have otherwise smelled it at the diner. And trust me, that's not a smell an 18-year-old would wear, Mom. Brianna's more of a DKNY perfume. The whispering got clearer once 'she' appeared, even though it was fading in and out, and then I heard it plain as day. I mean, I don't know, it's possible that I did smell the perfume and freaked out. You're right, it totally could have been my imagination. Either way, though, it made me feel super weird – like... sad – and I don't know how I'm gonna sleep tonight," Anna screwed up her face.

"Well, that's understandable, honey, but just try and refocus your mind on something more positive, like Boston. Please do me a favor and stay away from that place. You shouldn't be playing around with those types of things, especially if it's affecting you like this," her mom said as she reached over and held Anna's hand.

"You're right. I'm not going to go back there ever again. And I'm going to chalk this up to my imagination. Thanks for listening to me, Mom, and for being so cool about it." Anna smiled as she gave her mom a big hug.

"Good. Let's finish *Wives*. It's super juicy this episode," her mom pressed the pause button and they sank back into the couch to watch the drama unfold on-screen.

The next morning, Anna, Jay, and Abbey arrived at school thirty minutes before the first class was due to begin. Anna wanted to make sure she got to spend some time with her friends and Boston before her first class.

"Anna, I still can't get over your story from last night. That's incredible! Did Brianna just totally F-R-E-A-K? That would be kinda amazing to watch. You guys should have recorded it on your phone," Abbey answered in excitement.

"So, Brianna aside... are you still weirded out by the whole thing?" asked Jay.

"I don't know. It all seems totally surreal now, as if I just dreamed it all. I've never seen anything like that in my whole life. I'm sure once I've been at school for a while, I'll be able to shake the feeling off, and I will feel more normal. Then I can just file it away as a memory," sighed Anna.

Instantaneously her sigh turned into a big grin when she watched Boston's car pull up next to hers. "Woot woo... your boyfriend's here!" teased Jay.

"That's my other piece of news. He's officially MY boyfriend!" Anna beamed with excitement.

"Wait, what?! Guess Boston moves fast when he knows he has a good thing. Congrats, Anna!" shouted Abbey as she flung her arms around Anna's neck. "Girrrrl... Brianna's going to be sooo pissed! Ha ha!" she hissed.

"Stoppp... I don't even want to think about her—she's the one who coerced me into going to that house last night. Totally over hanging out with her ever again," replied Anna. The threesome stepped out of Anna's car. Boston immediately walked over to Anna.

"Hey, babe," he said, planting a quick kiss on her lips, giving her bottom lip a gentle tug with his teeth as he pulled away slowly but kept his arms draped around her waist.

"Hi," he smiled again. "Did you sleep okay?"

Anna felt warm still from the sexy nibble on her lip. Pulling herself together and clearing her throat, she answered, "Better than

I thought I would, honestly. What about you?"

"Well, I slept fine too, once I had my head under my covers," he joked.

"Ohh, poor boy!" Anna said while pecking him on his lips; one kiss just wasn't enough to start her day off with. *I don't think I could ever get bored of doing that!* she thought to herself and smiled.

"Jeez, get a room, you two," teased Abbey.

"Hey, Abbey, what's up?" laughed Boston as he let go of Anna.

"Well, my night paled in comparison to y'all's, apparently!"

"Hey Boston, you guys ready for the big game this week?" asked Jay.

"Yeah, man, I think so." With that, Boston and Jay immersed themselves into a deep conversation about the upcoming football game against Gettysburg.

"Anna!" Abbey hurried over to Anna and slid her arm through Anna's; "Did you get a chance to speak to Boston about Justin's current status?" asked Abbey in anticipation.

"I did. It's a bit of a bummer, Abs, but it sounds like he's taken." Anna screwed up her nose.

"Ugh, that sucks. By who?!" pouted Abbey.

"Ha! Just joking!" Anna burst into laughter. "He's single and ready to mingle! I told Boston not to say anything, but I can't promise that he won't. Seems like he thinks Justin might be into you. I kinda hope he does tell Justin. It will speed things up for you two. Then we can double date!" Anna grinned with excitement.

"Ummm, I'd rather he didn't do that. I'd rather just let things play out on their own organically, but whatever." Anna could tell that Abbey was trying to play it cool, but Anna knew that she was stoked.

Anna suddenly realized that she was wearing the same black jeans from the night before to school. *Can't believe I did that*, she thought to herself during Algebra II class.

Anna, like every other high school girl, understands the fashion faux pas of wearing the same dress, pants, skirt, etc. two days in a row. Anna pushed her hand inside of her pants pocket as she does when she gets bored and felt something inside of her pockets that she didn't expect. "Hmm, what's that?" she whispered as she pulled out what thought was a piece of string then realized it was a piece of yellow ribbon. "What the fu—!" she said out loud.

Everyone in the class, including Mr. Hall, turned and stared. "Anna, everything quite alright?" asked her teacher.

Anna looked up shocked, realizing she said that aloud. "Um yes... sorry, Mr. Hall." Anna felt her face turning red with embarrassment.

Boston looked over. "What's wrong?" he mouthed.

"Look" she whispered and held up the frayed and dirty piece of faded yellow ribbon.

Boston looked at the ribbon and then looked at Anna, "What?" He shook his head.

Turning both of her palms out the side, eyes wide, she replied, "I have no idea where this would have come from," she frowned. Boston shrugged his shoulders, not comprehending where Anna's mind was going with this discovery. Anna shook her head back at Boston, dismissing him. "Tell you after class," she whispered.

For the remainder of the class, Anna sat twiddling the ribbon between her fingers and trying to figure out where it would have come from, refusing to acknowledge her subconscious thoughts of what seemed to be the only logical, yet completely illogical, explanation.

After class, Boston and Abbey followed Anna to her locker. "What was that all about, Anna?" asked Abbey.

"Yeah, what's going on?" added Boston.

"I have no idea where this yellow ribbon came from! I just think it's super strange. I have not been around <u>any</u> ribbon, let alone this old yellow stuff. I'm serious, there is no reason at all why it would be in there. I'm trying not to jump to conclusions, and I know I'm being a bit paranoid, but I can't help but think about our night at the house."

"Anna, before you think of that, just call your mom. Maybe it got in there from the washing machine or something," Abbey said, trying to sound reasonable.

"I just really don't think it would be that; we don't even have ribbon at home. I don't know... I guess I will check in with her," replied Anna, feeling uneasy. "I'm sorry that I'm being an idiot. When I found the ribbon, it just made me think of the rhyme, 'Until yellow ribbons, ribbons, ribbons.' Just creeped me out a little bit is all."

"That is super weird, but I'm sure there's a good explanation," replied Abbey.

"Yep, I'm sure you guys are right," Anna smiled.

"Well, let us know what you find out," added Boston.

CHAPTER NINE

Friday afternoon came around sooner than expected. Boston stood by Anna's locker wanting to discuss the ribbon, while Anna had tried to put it out of her mind all week but failed miserably. When Anna just shook her head and looked down at her books, Boston changed the subject.

"Well, I have to go and get ready for the game tonight. You will be watching tonight, right?" asked Boston with a warm smile.

"Yes, of course! Good luck!" Anna replied as Boston leaned in and kissed her.

"See you later, babe. Bye, Abbey!" shouted Boston, seeing Abbey approach as he headed down the hallway.

"Go get 'em!" Abbey shouted back. She then turned to Anna and caught the faraway look in her eyes. "What's going on, Anna?"

"So, I haven't asked my mom yet about the ribbon because part of me doesn't want to know and the other part of me can't be bothered to explain it if she starts asking me questions."

Abbey knew how practical Anna could be about things, but the fact that the yellow ribbon wasn't in Anna's pocket the night before, instead somehow turning up in her pocket the next day, really did creep Abbey out, even if she downplayed it to Anna.

"So, I'll be honest, it is totally weird, Anna. Do you think there is any way that Brianna could have slipped it into your pocket when you were at the house to mess with you and be a biatch?"

"I don't think so, and I'm sure that I would have felt it. I mean, they are skinny jeans. But I guess that's always a possibility. I just don't think she would have had the chance, and I'm fairly sure that Boston would have seen it too," replied Anna. The two girls began walking down the hallway to the school's exit.

"Hey, are you going home before the game, or do you want to go grab a coffee first?" asked Abbey trying to take Anna's mind off of the ribbon.

"I could go for a cozy, warm coffee. I need to just call my mom and let her know my plans. Maybe I'll nonchalantly ask her quickly about the ribbon." As the girls arrived outside of Starbucks, Anna put her car in park and dialed her mom.

"Hi Anna!" her mom answered through Anna's car stereo.

"Mom! Can you take me off speakerphone? I can barely hear you with all the noise you're making!" shouted Anna back.

"Sorry, darling. I'm trying to get dinner ready," she replied while picking up the phone. "What's happening?"

"Mom, I was wondering if you had any yellow ribbon in the house? Or if you washed my jeans the other day with something that had yellow ribbon attached to it?"

"No, not that I can think of. Why?"

"No reason. But you're 100% sure that there's no yellow ribbon lying around?" Anna asked nervously.

"Yeah, honey, I'm positive." Anna looked nervous.

"Okay, thanks. By the way, Abbey and I are grabbing a coffee before the football game tonight, and don't forget that I'm hanging out with Boston after the game."

"Yep, I figured you would be watching the game. Have fun, love you!" replied her mom.

"Love you too, Mom," Anna said as she hit the 'End' button on her steering wheel. Anna and Abbey looked at each other dumbfounded.

"Maybe another explanation?" Abbey said hopefully with raised eyebrows.

"I don't think there is, Abs. I think it somehow came from Mary's house. Ugh, my stomach is so nervous it's making me feel sick," Anna replied with her face flushing red from anxiety. *What does this mean? Did she somehow put it in my pocket?* Anna thought to herself. *Don't be ridiculous, Anna, that's impossible. You're insane!*

"Can I ask you a stupid question? And then I'll drop it?" asked Abbey. "Don't freak out, but what if Mary Mack did somehow get that ribbon in your pocket?"

"I don't know. I mean, what if she did? What does that mean? Did she do it to scare me - to prove to me that she was really there and that she is real or what?"

"Anna, calm your beans. I guess we don't know and may never know why. I think you should just forget about it and just not talk about it anymore. Like you said, we have no idea how it got in there or why you have it. So just don't think about it anymore," advised Abbey reassuringly.

"Yeah, you're right. I think I will just do that! I'll start by thinking about how hot Boston will look in his uniform tonight, and he'll look even better now that he's all mine!" Anna teased as she shrilled with excitement.

"Ohhh yeah!" Abbey laughed back. With that, Anna threw the ribbon in her handbag, got out of her car, and walked into Starbucks.

I wonder how Jay's date with Becky is going? Anna pondered while reading the Starbucks menu. Becky and Jay had known each other since junior high, but were always just friends up until September, not long after the fall semester began. The two had always been attracted to each other, but for some reason they had always kept their relationship in the friendship zone. That was, until Jay and Becky started spending a lot of time together over the summer while working as lifeguards at Cannon Falls Country Club.

"Go, Napoleons, go! Go Napoleons!!" screamed Anna and Abbey as they waved their high school flags in the air. The score was 14–10 in favor of the Napoleons with 15 seconds left on the clock.

"If they can just defend our position, you and Boston will have some serious celebrating to do this weekend!" Abbey said while poking Anna in her arm.

"Umm hmmm, yes we will," Anna smirked.

"Anna! I've never seen you look so devilish before," laughed Abbey as she pulled the tartan blanket up farther over her legs to pad herself against the chill.

"Look, there's Jay and Becky!" Abbey said with excitement as she waved at Jay and beamed. Abbey liked to tease Jay as if he were her younger brother. Jay just acknowledged by nodding his head in annoyance. The crowd was going crazy. If they win this game, they would have defeated Gettysburg for the 4th year in a row, being the longest-reigning champions in the region. This game was a huge deal.

"Come on guys!" Anna screamed. Suddenly the ball was in Boston's hands, and he was running down the field. He caught the ball near the 50-yard line, and he was running fast, dodging the opposing team's defenders... 40 yards... 30 yards... 20 yards. "Go Boston! You can do it!" Anna screamed with excitement. Finally, he reached the end zone. "Touchdown!"

"Yessss!" screamed Abbey. The crowd went wild as the last 2 seconds ran out on the clock. The Napoleons had beaten the Gettysburg Pistols 21–13. Boston was charged by his fellow teammates as they threw their arms around him. The cheerleaders were doing backflips and throwing their pompoms high up into the air.

The football team finally broke apart and formed into a line as they made their way over to the center of the field to shake hands with their defeated opponents. The Napoleons prided themselves in being gracious and respectful, no matter if they win or lose. Shortly after, the crowd began charging the field as the Pistols exited the field.

Boston looked around as Anna and Abbey ran onto the field along with everybody else. Anna ran in-between people searching for Boston. She couldn't wait to throw her arms around him and give him a big kiss. Suddenly, Boston spotted Anna and ran toward her. Anna threw her arms around his neck. "Wow! Boston you were amazing! I'm so happy for you!" she beamed.

Boston moved his head to face Anna. "Thanks for coming to watch me play, babe. I really wanted to make you proud," he said, still panting from the sprint.

"Well, you did just that. I can't tell you how excited I am for you," she replied. "But you were showing off just a little, right?" Anna smiled.

"Umm, just a little bit, of course," he laughed, holding up his thumb and index finger showing measurement. Boston leaned in and kissed what felt like the life out of her, his adrenaline running overtime. "So, instead of going to Eddie's tonight, why don't we try somewhere different?" asked Boston after pulling away.

"Really? Are you sure? I know all of your teammates will be going there. I figured you would want to celebrate with them," Anna said shocked.

"I really just don't want to deal with Brianna and her groupies tonight."

"Well, the only thing is that I came here with Abs, so she'll be coming with us too."

"That won't be a problem. I had already mentioned something to Justin about the four of us going to Cannons for dinner and a game of pool," Boston said inquisitively.

"Hmm, very clever, Mr. Tate. Abs will be thrilled - maybe a little embarrassed - but totally stoked. That was very nice of you to do that," Anna exclaimed while giving Boston another big hug. "Let me go tell her. She's over there talking to Jay. Shall we meet you there?"

"Sounds good! We obviously need to hit the showers first. I can be there in like 30 minutes?" he asked while removing his hands from her waist.

"Perf! See you soon then. Congrats again! You really did great!" Anna said while quickly planting a peck on his lips.

Making her way over to where Jay, Abbey, and Becky stood talking,

Anna passed Brianna who had been unnaturally quiet about the whole Mack House interaction. Anna figured that she must be really freaked out about the whole thing and was choosing to act like it didn't happen. For the first time in her life, Brianna had finally been shut up by someone or something. Brianna looked at Anna and coldly said 'hi'. Anna was fine with the extremely brief exchange. "Hey," she replied while giving her a cracked smile.

"Abs!" shouted Anna as she got closer, beaming with excitement. "Abs, I have something super exciting to tell you!" she exclaimed mischievously.

"Anna, what is that look about?" she asked intrigued.

"Hey Jay... hi Becky! You guys enjoyed the game?" asked Anna.

"It was a great game for a first date," laughed Jay.

"Yeah, no kidding! Totes exciting!!" Becky added.

"So, did you see your boyfriend yet?" asked Jay.

"Yep. He was obviously really stoked. Not sure he could have smiled any bigger," Anna said with a smile.

"Understandable. Tell him I said congrats!" Jay then turned to Becky. "You ready to head out before the line in the parking lot gets too crazy?" Jay asked while putting his arm around her.

"Sure, that sounds like a good idea. Bye, Anna! Bye, Abbey!" Becky smiled widely.

"Bye, guys. Have fun tonight!" Anna shouted as they turned and walked away.

∞

"Okay, Abs, don't freak out, because this is super short notice, and it's just a casual dinner"

"Spill it, Anna," Abbey said sharply.

"Okay. But... Boston just told me that he wants to go to Cannons to eat dinner and play pool, and he doesn't want to have to deal with Brianna and crew tonight."

"Okay... and? Go on," Abbey interrupted.

"Well, he just told me that Justin is coming with us!" Anna said as her eyes widened with excitement.

"WTF?! OMG, Anna, are you guys trying to set us up on a double date or something?"

"No, Abs. Honestly, I knew nothing about it, I swear. Boston just told me that Justin was coming with us. He didn't say that it was a double date or anything like that. He simply just said that Justin is coming with us." Anna said while grabbing Abbey's arm reassuringly.

"Ugh, whatev... it's fine. Let's just get going. This is going to be super awkward but exciting!" Abbey beamed. "I can't say it's not a little nerve wracking, and you know I have control issues, but I am excited about it. Now I need to freshen up."

"Well, like I said, Boston just doesn't want to be around the usual group tonight," Anna replied.

"Okay... okay. It's getting really cold outside. Can we get going?" Abbey asked while linking her arm through Anna's.

"Seriously though, do we have time to stop by my house really quick? I just want to touch up my makeup." asked Abbey.

"Yeah, of course! Boston said they need like 30 minutes," Anna said, recollecting how just three short weeks ago she sounded just like Abbey.

Anna and Abbey sang along to Taylor Swift on the radio as they headed to the restaurant after stopping at Abbey's house. "Holy cow! Is that Boston's car? How in the heck did they beat us here? I thought for sure we would get here before them," Anna said in surprise.

"I did probably take longer than I should have to freshen up," snorted Abbey with laughter.

"That's okay. You want to look irresistible to Justin. I get it," laughed Anna.

"Heck yeah!" Abbey agreed.

"Are you getting nervous yet?" Anna poked.

"No Anna, just ready to get inside so I can sit down and check him out, LOL."

"I know you're not joking, and I am here for it!" laughed Anna.

As the girls walked into the restaurant, they spotted Justin and Boston standing near the white brick fireplace and quite a few other people standing around the bar. "Um, god, he looks freakin' hot!" said Abbey calmly to Anna, attempting to play it cool in front of Justin.

"Hey, babe! Hey, Abbey!" said Boston.

"Hey... is there much of a wait?" asked Anna.

"Not too bad. We just got here. They said it would be about 20 minutes," Justin chimed in.

"The fire feels really good, actually. It's freakin' chilly out there now. I think they said it was one of the coldest nights so far this season," Anna said while shifting closer to Boston. He responded by rubbing both her arms up and down.

"Congrats on the win, Justin, super exciting!" Abbey smiled.

"Thanks Abs... we're still buzzing about it. Four years in a row! That's gotta sting for the Pistols," Justin laughed.

"Yeah, no kidding!" smiled Abbey.

A few moments later, the hostess called Boston's name.

"Ahh... I'm starving!" Boston announced.

"Boston, party of 4?" questioned the older woman with blonde curly hair.

"That's us!" Boston replied.

"Hey Justin! How are you? We have a booth for you, is that okay?" she smiled.

"Perfect, Mrs. Livingston," Justin replied graciously; seemingly, the woman knew Justin and he knew her.

"Great! Please follow me," she said while grabbing four menus from the holder on the wall beside her. The hostess then turned and led the group toward their table. The woman appeared to be in her late fifties but had a very young-looking face and was wearing all black clothes that looked expensive and very well put together.

"You all enjoy your dinner, and you boys be gentlemen - especially you, Justin," she jested, pointing her finger at Justin.

"Of course, Mrs. Livingston!" Justin chuckled.

"Great job tonight, boys. No doubt Mr. Livingston will be out here soon to congratulate you all and shake your hands," she beamed and walked away.

"How do you know her, Justin?" asked Boston.

"Oh, my parents have known her for years. She and Mr. Livingston used to come over for dinner now and again. They own this place," he replied.

"Oh wow, that's cool. She still acts as the hostess?" asked Abbey.

"Well, she doesn't need to, but she hosts a few nights a week. Mrs. Livingston used to do it every night when they first opened, and she still likes to keep in touch with the customers."

"Wow, that's pretty cool of her," Anna added.

"Yeah. I can see by the ring on her finger that she obviously doesn't need to work," laughed Abbey.

"No... she does not. But they're both very down-to-earth. Mr. Livingston is a super funny dude," Justin laughed back.

"What are you all getting to eat? I'm going to just eat myself stupid tonight and get the triple quarter pounder BBQ burger and fries," Boston said while licking his lips.

"Wow, you are quite excited about that," laughed Anna.

"Yep. After a game like tonight, I could eat a horse," Boston replied.

"Ah that sounds good man, think I will get the same but minus the BBQ sauce," Justin said while closing his menu.

"Hmm, I'm going to get the turkey burger and coleslaw," Anna stated.

"Not me. I love their chicken strips with mac and cheese, y-u-m-m!" Abbey moaned.

"Wow, someone is getting excited. I'm feelin' pretty jealous of the food right now," Justin squinted his eyes, smiling.

Abbey blushed slightly as she thought of a flirty, witty comeback. "Oh Justin, don't be so jelly. I'm sure you could find a way to make me equally as excited." Abbey paused, then added, "Like buying me an ice cream for dessert!" she giggled.

Anna couldn't help but chuckle, *the girl has no shame*, she laughed to herself.

"Ha! Good one, Abs," laughed Justin. Abbey always had a knack for witty comeback lines.

"Actually, I've changed my mind. I'm going to get the triple quarter pound Philly cheesesteak sandwich with fries," Boston confirmed while placing his menu down on the table as the waitress approached.

CHAPTER TEN

"So, what are your plans for tomorrow, Anna?" asked Boston. "Umm, going shopping with my mom in the afternoon, and Abbey and I were thinking about going to a movie or something like that. But I'm not really sure yet," she replied. *Please ask me to hang out*, Anna's mind begged.

"Okay, so a girls' night thing?" asked Boston.

"Eh, not really, just a casual night?" Anna questioned Abbey.

"Yeah. No... like Anna said, nothing's set in stone yet."

"Okay," Boston said enthusiastically. "So the Fall Festival downtown starts tomorrow. I imagine you girls go to that, right?" he asked.

"OMG, of course! I love the fall season and Halloween time. We always go," replied Anna.

Cannon Falls is famous in the state of Pennsylvania for their fall festival, which dates back to 1900. Tourists come from hundreds of miles to gather at the festival to eat food, drink, listen to music, and enjoy the Halloween festivities which include Pumpkin carving and caramel apple contests. The fall festival lasts through the month of October and is one of the town's biggest events aside from the Holiday Festival in December.

"Cool... well, do you mind if I tag along with you ladies?" asked Boston.

"Of course, we were going to see if Jay wanted to hang out too," smiled Anna. Abbey was hoping that Justin would hang out also, but he didn't mention anything during dinner.

After dinner, Anna and Abbey went to the restroom. "Are you enjoying yourself, Abs?" Anna poked Abbey in the ribs playfully.

"Yeah! Justin is being super nice, and he really is totally my type," Abbey beamed.

"He's definitely flirting with you. He's made a couple of comments now. I think he likes you. You should ask him to come along tomorrow," Anna insisted.

"I don't know. I don't want to look too eager. Besides, Justin's kind of a flirty guy to begin with. I'm just going to play it cool and see where it goes," Abbey said while putting on lipstick.

"God, I feel sooo disgustingly full," Anna said while looking at her stomach in the mirror and adjusting her shirt. "Ugh... so bloated!"

"Oh whatevs! Shut up, Anna. You're crazy!"

"LOL. Yeah, but still, there's no way I could manage dessert," replied Anna.

"Well, you know me, I can always squeeze in a little dessert," laughed Abbey.

As the girls headed back to the table, the waitress was just leaving their booth.

"Oh hey, did you girls want anything else? You just missed her." said Boston.

"Maybe," Abbey confirmed.

"She'll be back in a couple of minutes to refill our drinks." Minutes later, the waitress returned with three dishes: a brownie, apple pie, and a plate with two scoops of ice cream placed carefully on top of a salted caramel cookie. "Thought we could split dessert," smiled Boston. The waitress sat the dishes down on the table, placing the bowl of ice cream in front of Abbey.

"Oh my gosh!" Abbey and Anna laughed out loud.

"Well... you did say you loved dessert," Justin smirked.

"You are too funny, Justin. I have no doubt that you can tackle all of this," Abbey nudged him in the stomach.

After dessert, the foursome headed over to the pool table. "Girls against guys?" asked Abbey.

"Sure! You sound pretty confident," chuckled Justin. After playing the best of three, the guys had beaten Abbey and Anna two to one.

"Why don't we play Justin and Abbey against Anna and me?" questioned Boston.

"Sure! Maybe you'll get to win this round, Abbey" smiled Justin. "If that's okay with you, I mean?" he added.

"Ouch, jerk. That's fine with me," she smiled.

After playing another set of three, Abbey and Justin won two to one also. "Ouch, that's got to sting, dude!" Justin joked.

"Yeah whatevs... just didn't want to ruin your date night," Boston hit back.

"Wow... its eleven o'clock, I need to get going home, Abbey," Anna said, looking at her watch.

"Ugh, yeah we do!"

"Here, we'll walk you ladies out. I'm ready to go home and crash." The exhaustion from the football game was starting to hit Boston. Anna and Boston held hands and walked ahead of Abbey and Justin.

"Thanks again for setting this up for Abs. I hope he had fun hanging out with us?"

"Yeah, he did. I really think he likes Abbey."

"Really? That's awesome! Well, I guess we'll see what happens," Anna said with excitement while squeezing Boston's hand. As

Anna and Boston arrived at her car, she unlocked her car door and opened it.

"So, I'll see you tomorrow for the festival?" asked Boston.

"I'm really looking forward to it. I'll call you tomorrow, and we can figure out the logistics," Anna confirmed.

"Cool, goodnight. It was nice to have a more normal night with you," he smiled as he leaned in and kissed her.

Mmmmm, Anna relished the kiss. Meanwhile, Justin and Abbey talked quietly as they approached the car.

"So, you guys are definitely going to the festival tomorrow. That should be a good time," stated Justin.

"Yeah, it will be fun."

"I was thinking of maybe tagging along with you," Justin hinted.

"You totally should," Abbey said encouragingly.

"Would you like to go to the festival with me as a double date?" asked Justin nervously.

"Umm... yeah. That would be great!" Abbey said a little shocked. "I think Jay might come along too, but I think he's bringing Becky with him."

"Jay's a cool guy," replied Justin.

Abbey climbed into the passenger seat of Anna's car.

"See you tomorrow, Abs." Justin smiled as he reached to close her door.

"Alright, have a good night, Justin," Abbey beamed back.

Anna finally got into the car and closed the door. "I hate to watch him go, but I looove to watch him leave," Anna said, bursting into laughter as she watched Boston walk toward his car, wearing his dirty blue jeans and football jacket.

"OMG, Anna, you're a total nerd!!" screamed Abbey as she laughed hysterically. "Welllll, I have some fun news of my own," Abbey added after she stopped giggling.

"Really? Do tell," Anna replied. Abbey proceeded to tell her best friend the exciting news.

"OMG, Abs, that's freakin' awesome, Woo hoo! Tomorrow will be so much fun!" exclaimed Anna.

"I know, I can't wait!"

"We need to call Jay and tell him about the double date tomorrow and see if he wants to join us," said Abbey.

"For sure, it would be fun to do a triple date," Anna replied. "Hopefully, he will go," she added.

"I'm really happy for you though, Anna. You really deserve this. I mean this relationship, it suits you. You seem really happy, and I really like Boston."

"Thanks, Abs, I am really happy with Boston. I just hope it keeps getting better."

Anna's eyes pricked up as her car headed down 106 toward the Mack House. Anna slowed her car down.

"You still thinking about that, Anna?" asked Abbey.

"Yep, I just can't shake it. I don't know what to do. Part of me wants to go there and figure it all out. But part of me thinks it's just spooky, and I should just leave it alone. I don't know. I just want to look in the window as we go by, just to see if I see anything."

"Are you sure? What if you see something? It might freak you out all over again," Abbey suggested.

"I don't know. I just can't shake the feeling that I need to do this," Anna replied nervously as her stomach continued to follow suit and cramp from the anxiety of seeing the house again. The house looked just as it did before. The windows were dark, and the shadows from the ivy crept across the exterior walls.

"Brrrr," Abbey shuddered. "I still can't believe that you went in there at night! There's no way! I would have been so s-c-a-r-e-d," Abbey hissed.

"I wish I hadn't, trust me," Anna shook her head. The house was closer now, and Anna's car crept along the dark road. Anna leaned forward over the steering wheel, squinting her eyes trying to see if there was any movement from inside the house.

"Hmm, what's that over there?" asked Abbey.

"Where?"

"By the side of her house."

"Where? I can't see what you're talking about," Anna said sharply.

"Right freakin' there!" Abbey said as she pointed her finger to something wrapped around one of a tree's larger branches.

"Holy Shhh—!" Anna said as she finally caught sight of what Abbey was talking about.

"Oh my gosh!" Abbey said confused, as she squinted her eyes trying to make sense of what she was seeing. Anna automatically swerved her car over to the parking lot at the front of the house. "Anna, are you crazy! What are you doing?" Abbey gasped.

"I have to take a closer look, Abs."

"Anna, are you sure? That's too creepy!" Abbey shuddered.

"Yes, and I want you to get out with me... please?" Anna begged.

"God! Anna, I won't. I'm not, ugh, whatever... fine." Abbey shook her head. "But you better make this quick. I can't believe we are doing this late at night," Abbey snorted as she opened up her car door when Anna came to a complete stop.

Anna stepped out of her car. "Thanks, Abs. I owe you one," she said as she walked around to Abbey's side of the car and linked her arm around hers. "Come on, this will only take a second," she added. As the two girls walked up to the big oak tree that had already lost most of its leaves to the fall season, the object hanging from the tree became more apparent.

"Well, that is super weird!" Abbey whispered. Anna reached her hand toward the branch and touched the faded yellow shabby ribbon that was tied around it.

"I don't know what to say. I know I hadn't seen it before. It definitely wasn't here last week, yet it looks like it's been here for years!"

Anna reached into her handbag and pulled out the yellow ribbon she found in her pocket a few days earlier. She held it up to the ribbon hanging on the tree. "It matches exactly... down to the dirt stains and fading, Abs."

"Unbelievable. I just can't make any sense of it," she replied. "I feel like someone is trying to get my attention," Anna added.

Anna and Abbey both looked across the lawn to the house. "You know... I can't believe I'm about to say this—at all. But I think you are right, Anna. But I don't think 'someone' is, Anna. I think, specifically, Mary is trying to get your attention," she said while squeezing Anna's arm tightly.

"Let's get back to the car. It's freezing, and I'm thoroughly creeped out now," Anna replied. Anna sped away from the house fairly quickly and sat silent just driving and not saying a word.

"Anna, are you okay?" Abbey asked in concern. "I mean, I know you are just totally weirded out now and all, but you are okay, right? You haven't said a peep."

Anna inhaled and exhaled slowly. "Sorry. I'm just freaked out, and I just can't believe we just saw that... I'm trying to rationalize it, but I can't. I'll be fine though."

"So, let me ask you this. Are you going to do anything about it or just try to let it all go?" Abbey asked, trying to not sound as if she was pressuring her.

"I don't know, Abs. Part of me, in a strange way, feels bad

ignoring it, but this is just way over my head, and it's plain surreal."

"Well, for what it's worth, here are my two cents. I don't think you can ignore it anymore. I think for peace of mind that you need to try and figure out what's going on. I don't know, maybe call a psychic or something."

"I'm going to sleep on it. I just keep thinking about her crying, and it makes me feel bad for her. And I'm not calling a psychic. That's just... I don't know... strange," Anna said as they pulled into Abbey's driveway.

"Well, yeah, you should think about it. Maybe talk to Boston about it. See what he thinks you should do," Abbey suggested as she unbuckled her seatbelt.

"Maybe. We'll see. See you tomorrow!" Anna replied.

As soon as Anna got home, she ran into the house to tell her mom what happened, but both her mom and dad lay sleeping on the couch in front of *CSI Miami* playing on the television in the background.

She felt bad when thinking about waking her mom up so she went into the kitchen and got herself Oreos and milk, her favorite late-night snack, and headed up to her bedroom. Once in her room, she flicked on her flat-screen TV and turned it to the VH1 channel. "A little bit of normal," she said to herself out loud, still trying to shake the bizarre sequence of events that had occurred in the past week.

As she looked down at her phone to check the time, a text message from Boston appeared.

"U still awake?"

Anna stared at her phone. *Ugh, I have so much to tell him, too much to say via text*, she concluded. Anna clicked away at the mini keypad on her iPhone.

"Yep just got home. Now watchin tv"

"Cool. Wish we cud watch tv 2gether ;-)"

"Me 2. What r u doin?"

"Tryin 2 find somthin 2 binge on Netflix"

"Gotcha. Abs told me Justin wants 2 dble d8 with us 2morrow"

"Yeah he told me 2. Will b good!"

"Can't wait! Sooo... made a pitstop at Mary's house which turned interesting"

"What! Why?"

"Too much 2 tell u. Talk 2morrow"

"Tell me now x"

"No 2morrow :)"

As she was typing a cheeky response, her phone rang. "God, he's so impatient," Anna laughed to herself. She quickly answered it, as she didn't want her parents to hear her phone at that time of night; it was past her phone curfew. "Hello Mr. Impatient," Anna teased.

"Hey, babe. So why did you stop by the house? I thought you weren't going to go back there again?"

"I wasn't planning on it, but you won't believe what I'm about to tell you," Anna exclaimed.

After finishing her story, Boston was speechless. "Holy crap" were the only two words out of his mouth.

"I know, right?! Needless to say, I'm totally freaked out!" Anna rested her hand on her forehead.

"Well, I talked to Mark, and he said it scared the crap out of Brianna. She won't even talk about it anymore. He did manage to find out about the perfume. She said she didn't notice anything like that, except for the old smokey fireplace smell. I didn't ask him about if she heard anything 'cause you told me not to bring it up. But I assume she didn't, otherwise he would have told me. So, it sounds like you were the only one who could smell it."

"Thanks! That's not super comforting," Anna scoffed.

"So, what are you going to do?" asked Boston.

"I don't know. I guess I'm just going to sleep on it. I'll figure something out."

"Good idea. But if you do decide to pursue it, I want you to know that I'll help you. I don't want you to have to do this all by yourself," Boston assured her.

"Thanks, that's what Abs told me too. I'm sure that Jay will try to convince me to look into this further also," Anna sighed.

"Well, it's your decision, but for what it's worth, if I were you, I think the curiosity would most definitely kill the cat," Boston chuckled.

"Yeah, we'll see. I'm getting sleepy though, so I'm gonna get go to bed now. I'll call you tomorrow, Mr. Tate."

"Okay, sweet dreams, Anna."

"Hmm, you too. You did great today." Anna smiled softly.

"Thanks, babe. Goodnight." Boston ended the call.

CHAPTER ELEVEN

Anna woke up to the sound of her mom using the electric whisk, beating up what Anna would guess to be pancake batter. She stretched her arms high above her head as she sat up in bed. She checked the time on her phone; "Jeez... 9:30. I must have been really tired," she said to herself.

Then her thoughts wandered to Boston. *I'll give it till 10:30, and then I'll text him about the festival. I'm sure he's sleeping in today*, she thought to herself as she pictured Boston looking for her in the crowd the day before in his muddy uniform. Anna jumped out of bed. She could hear the dogs' collars jingling as they ran up the stairs to greet her good morning. "Hi puppies!" she said while petting them both on their heads. "Breakfast then outfit," she said to them.

With that, she ran downstairs to make sure she didn't miss out on Saturday's pancake and sausage special, another one of her mom's traditions. "Good morning, darling!" she smiled. "Tell me all about your night last night. Are you seeing him again?" she quizzed.

"Yes, of course! It was good..." Anna continued to recount the date and Abbey's exciting news to her mom.

"That's fantastic! How fun!" she said while laying a large golden pancake on Anna's plate. "Abbey must be thrilled, and it's always fun to double date," she smiled. "Is he a nice boy?" Her mom asked concerned.

"Yeah, Justin's a good guy, and Abs is super excited," Anna assured. Anna tossed around the idea of telling her mom what she and Abbey got up to after dinner at Mary's house the night before, but she wasn't sure if now was the right time. After contemplating it further, she decided not to, as Anna wasn't even sure herself yet if it was worth discussing or if she was even going to pursue the whole thing.

"You seem a bit preoccupied, Anna, is everything okay?" asked Boston as he watched her play with the straw in her glass of coke while she stared at some trees in the small, black iron-gated park on Main Street.

Anna shook her head when she realized that she had completely spaced out. "Oh, ha! Yep, I'm fine, just thinking about a few things."

"Hmmm... can I pry? If I'm being nosey, you can tell me to butt out. I won't be offended," he teased with a tone of intrigue.

"Well, actually, there are a few things I'm thinking about, but I guess they are all really part of the same thing."

"Let me guess... Mary?"

"Correct. I feel like I sound like a broken record..."

Boston reached over the small round wooden table and took hold of Anna's hand. "Anna, I get it. I want you to feel like you can always talk to me. You can tell me anything. I'm never gonna judge you. Let's be real. This is a pretty crazy situation for you and any of us to be in. So, lay it on me," he said warmly.

What have I done to deserve you? Anna thought to herself. "Okay," she smiled. Anna took a deep breath. "So, obviously this whole thing with what happened last night just confuses me more. It's just all very surreal, and I don't know if I should just try and ignore it or dive in and try and make sense of it. Put on your PI hat. I kinda feel responsible in some weird way. Like, I feel bad for Mary, but it's also creepy and honestly a little scary at the same time. Selfishly, I don't want to think about it all, because I just want to concentrate on just being here with you and getting to know you more."

"See, that was quite a load off, huh?" Boston smiled. "Hmmm, a private investigator hat would look pretty sexy on you. Listen, clearly you have a lot on your mind, so let me just reiterate this: I want to help you if you choose to take it further. I get where you're coming from if you decide to let it go, but I think you are going to have a hard time ignoring it. You have a big heart, Anna, and I think it will drive you nuts not knowing why all of this happened. You may even feel guilty for ignoring her. Otherwise, you could make the decision right now to forget about it and let that be the end of it," Boston said while kissing her knuckles. Anna felt a tingle run all the way up arm and warmth spread across her face.

"Thank you... it means a lot that you would help me. In fact, I'm going to put it out of my mind for now, focus on our date, and decide tomorrow. Now, let's go find the others," Anna said as she stood up. She then pulled on Boston's arm, tugging him to his feet.

"All right, but not before I grab some kettle corn. I l-o-v-e that stuff!" Boston wrapped his arm around Anna's waist and pulled her in for a cheeky kiss.

God, you smell good! Anna breathed in Boston's Axe body spray.

"You seriously eat like a horse!" Anna jested. "Candy, fries, burger... you are a bottomless pit!" she added as she patted his stomach.

"Ha! It's all the football practice... and let's face it, I am a big pig," he laughed, leaning in and breathing in her hair before consuming her mouth in the gentlest way with his own. At that moment, Anna felt a warm sensation fill her stomach that made her shudder.

Strings of white and orange lights connecting one lamp post to another lined the streets. Silhouettes of witches on broomsticks decorated the tops of lampposts. Beer, wine, and food tents dotted the town square. Several apple cider and kettle corn stands were packed with those under 21 and parents with children.

A local band played in the background on the center stage at the old cannon pavilion. "I love this song!" Anna said as she hummed along. The band was playing John Mayer's "Half of My Heart."

Anna looked over her left shoulder as she watched a crowd dance along in front of the pavilion. "Want to go dance?" asked Boston as he noticed her watching them.

"Really?" she said surprised.

"What, 'cause I'm a football player, I can't dance?" he smirked.

"Whatevs. I'm just surprised that you would want to do that here when it's still a little light out," she said nonchalantly.

Boston grabbed Anna's hand and led her over to the front of the stage. As he pulled her in close with both arms wrapped around her waist, Anna rested her head on his chest. The moment seemed to freeze in time; she had never felt so happy. For the first time in her life, Anna felt like she was beginning to understand what falling in love meant. The logical side of her brain then kicked into gear: *Anna—it's been all of three weeks, don't get ahead of yourself!*

At that very moment, Boston reached down and placed the underneath of his index finger under her chin and gently pulled up her face to look at him as he leaned in for another kiss. *Oh god... what am I going to do with you*, Anna thought as a shiver ran down her spine and caused knots of excitement in her stomach to churn. As the song ended, Anna opened her eyes. "We really should go find the others. I'm sure Abs is wondering where we are."

"Lead the way," Boston gestured.

Finally, the couple found Abbey and Justin by the shopping booths. "Hey there!" Abbey said with a huge smile. "What have you guys been up to, hmmm?" she winked.

Anna rolled her eyes playfully. "Boston wanted to get some kettle corn and then we danced to the last half of the John Mayer song the band just played."

"Anyway, check out this little dangly thing I was thinking of getting for you to hang on your rear-view mirror, Anna," Abbey pointed to a small pendant necklace made of wood with a hand-painted black little witch riding on a broomstick. The words, 'The Witch Is In' were painted along the side of the broomstick in orange font.

"Oh ha ha... very funny, Abs!" Anna laughed.

"Yeah. Funny but true," she giggled while handing a $10 bill to the woman working at the Halloween-themed booth.

"That's actually pretty funny, Abbey!" laughed Justin.

"It really is. Where's Jay and Becky, by the way?" asked Boston.

"They went to go get some food," replied Abbey.

"So, what shall we do next?" asked Anna while looking out

over the festival grounds and contemplating their next move. Dusk had finally fallen, and the streetlamps of the park created a cozy glow among all the other Halloween lights from the booths and attractions.

"How about the haunted house?" asked Justin. "We haven't done that yet, and personally I will find it amusing to watch Abbey freak the hell out," he jested while putting his arm around her.

"Oh really? I have a feeling, dude, that you will be more of a chicken than me. And yeah, I would totes find that freakin' hilarious! Come on, Anna, let's see if these big, scary football players are as tough as they make out to be on the field." Abbey replied, linking her arm through Anna's and dragging her toward the haunted house. "I'd love me some haunted houses... fun times!" Abbey buzzed.

"You're such a nerd, Abs!" giggled Anna. "It's so weird to think this time last year we were all single, wandering around just the three of us in the haunted house. Who knew how different the festival would be this year..." Anna said quietly in Abbey's ear.

"I know, right, crazy. Ohhh, now there's a point, let me grab my phone and text Jay to see if he and Becky want to come meet us at the entrance. I'm sure there will be a line anyway."

A few seconds later, Anna heard the chiming bell tone coming from Abbey's purse, announcing a text message from Jay. "Oh cool, they're on their way over here now," Abbey added while looking around at the festival.

The group headed toward the waiting line in front of the

haunted house. Anna took note of some of the people's faces as they exited the attraction. One young red-headed girl who had to be no older than fourteen looked as pale as a ghost, her eyes wide with fright. What appeared to be her older brother walked next to her with his arm wrapped around her shoulder, comforting her. The boy who appeared to be about nineteen or twenty didn't do such a good job of hiding his amusement at the situation as he struggled to contain the grin on his face.

The screams and laughter from the big swings, Twister, electric cars, and the big wheel filled the air and echoed across the park. The smell of corn dogs, burgers, and fries lingered on the mildly cool fall evening breeze. "It is the cutest thing how they decorate the Main Street each year for this," Anna said to Boston.

"They do a really good job. It must take people ages to set this all up. Actually, it must have taken them about a week. I saw some of the big semi's roll into town last weekend carrying all the rides and attraction equipment."

"Hey guys!" announced Jay as he and Becky walked up behind the group to where they stood in line at the front of the haunted house.

As soon as the group got past the front door, they proceeded down a long, thin, dimly lit hallway. Strobe lights flickered on and off rapidly. Organ music played in the background with sounds of moans, screams, shots being fired, and chainsaws randomly interrupting the music. As the group turned a corner, they walked through another hallway that was shrouded in almost complete darkness, except for a small wooden table that had a red glowing lamp sitting on it at the end of the hallway. Illuminated above the table was a picture of a woman with only her shoulders, neck, and head visible in the picture. As Anna got closer, she realized that it was a portrait of Mary Mack. Anna could feel her cheeks flush with anxiety.

Boston turned to look at Anna as the group realized that this year's theme was clearly a play on the Mack House. "We can totally leave, if you want," asked Boston, understanding that this was really poorly timed, and there was a good chance that Anna felt uncomfortable.

Anna took in a deep breath. "No, it's okay. It's just a stupid haunted house anyway," she replied, trying to convince herself. Even though she had already made it inside, she wanted to scream and run away. Boston took hold of Anna's hand, pulled her in closely, and walked behind her. Abbey walked in front of Anna and behind Justin who led the way. Jay and Becky trailed behind Boston.

Abbey turned around to face Anna. "Wow... they really picked an original theme for Cannon Falls," she scoffed sarcastically.

As the group turned another corner, they were startled by a ghostly figure of a woman dressed in black with a pale white face. Her skin rippled with deep wrinkles as if she had recently risen from the grave. "Arghh!" screamed the girls.

Just hold on, Anna, this must be over soon, she cringed.

The group walked into another dimly lit room, almost pitch-black but with a moonlit glow coming from the full ceiling. Small, leafless trees with yellow ribbons wrapped around multiple branches and limbs filled the room.

Suddenly some Union and Confederate soldiers covered in blood jumped out from what seemed like nowhere and charged toward the group, holding their swords and rifles. One very unlikely soldier holding a chainsaw above his head rushed toward Anna her friends. This made the entire group jump and scream, shuffling forward as quickly as they could. After going through a couple more rooms, the group finally made it out of the back entrance of the haunted house. *Thank God!* Anna relaxed.

"Are you okay, Anna? That didn't totally freak you out too much, did it?" asked Jay sympathetically.

"I'm okay. I wish I would have known that was the theme, because I would have given it a miss. It's okay though. Did you have fun, Becky?" she asked.

"Yeah, that was super freaky!" laughed Becky without any knowledge of what Anna and Boston had experienced within the past week.

After a ride on the Ferris Wheel, the group felt like they were ready for a change of scenery. "Anyone up for going to Eddie's or to

Cannons?" asked Justin.

"Sounds good to me," replied Abbey enthusiastically. Boston looked at Anna for direction.

Anna nodded her head, "Sure. Eddies sounds good."

"I drove so, Abbey, do you want to ride with me?" asked Justin.

"For sure, I can do that," she grinned at Anna.

"Boston, do you want to ride with me then?" asked Anna.

"Yep," he replied simply.

"I think we're gonna give it a miss this time. But you guys have fun," added Jay.

"Okay, we'll see you later then," Abbey said while giving Jay a hug goodbye.

On the way to Eddie's, Anna drifted off thinking about everything, trying to confirm if the decision she had just made was the right one. "I think I know what I'm going to do," announced Anna.

"Really? What is it?" asked Boston.

"I'm going to do it. I'm going to figure this thing out. I want to understand why this is happening," she said confidently.

"Okay, so you're 100% sure this is what you want? What made you want to do it?" Boston said surprised.

"A couple of reasons. First, I feel bad about what happened to Mary and Benjamin. It's just so sad to think about how much pain she must have felt not knowing if he would ever come back. I just couldn't imagine how she lived with that." Deep down Anna knew how she felt about Boston, and they've only just started their relationship. "Second, I kinda hate how the haunted house today felt like they were making a mockery of their lives... like it was a joke. I want to help or whatever. I just still can't believe I'm even talking about this, that it is all a REAL thing."

"Cool! I'm glad you feel good about this, but promise me one thing?"

"What's that?"

"That you'll not do this by yourself. That you'll let me and others help you," he ordered.

"I would really like that," Anna replied without hesitation. Anna took a minute to reflect on how much her life had changed in the past 2 months. *Who would have thought that I would be solving this paranormal mystery, but also that I would be doing this with the help of my boyfriend, Boston Tate. Wild*, she thought to herself.

CHAPTER TWELVE

"I'm going to do some googling to see if I can find out any information online about the Mack House. You know, about experiences, or whatever, that maybe other people have reported on any tourist sites and stuff," Anna said while she flipped open her laptop. "I wonder if the Historical Society has noted anything about the house being haunted. I'll check that too," she added.

Abbey and Boston sat on the loveseat in Anna's bedroom the following Saturday, watching Anna sitting at her desk in anticipation of what she might find out online. "I can also do some searching on the Cannon Falls Herald website on my tablet to see what might be in their archive databases," said Abbey while pulling her iPad out of its case.

"Cool! That's a good idea," Anna replied happily. She was glad that Abbey and Boston were there to help and support her. They would help make things not feel so strange or creepy like it would be if she was on her own.

Just then Anna's mom popped her head into Anna's bedroom. "Hi guys, just wondered if you would like some grilled cheese sandwiches for lunch?" she asked with a grin.

"Oh, yes, please, Mrs. Ipswich. That sounds awesome. I love a good grilled cheese," Boston replied eagerly.

"Abbey?"

"Yesss, puhleez Mom," she replied, just as Abbey had addressed Anna's mom for years. Since she had known Anna's mom for most of her life, Mrs. Ipswich has been basically like Abbey's second mom.

"For sure, Mom," Anna unintentionally swatted her hand at her mom, almost shooing her away.

"Anna Ipswich, don't be so cheeky," her mom lightly snapped back.

"Sorry, Mom, I didn't mean to be! Love you! Thanks for the sandwiches!" Anna called out as her mom headed down the hallway to the stairs.

"Oh... oh... I found something, listen!" demanded Abbey. "This local article is dated from 1994. Apparently one of the Historical Society members, Carly Stein, who worked at the Mack House, was closing the place up one night when she started to smell a strange odor. Stein reported that she felt someone gently grab her elbow when she reached for the front door. The next minute she passed out, and her husband had to go to the Mack House to pick her up after Stein didn't arrive home when expected. Isn't that insane!" she exclaimed.

"Wow! That is super weird. Can you text me the link to that? I'd like to read the full article later," said Anna.

"Sure thing!"

Boston raised his eyebrows as he settled on an idea of his own. "Don't get mad at me for what I'm going to suggest, but how would you feel if I talked to Brianna alone tonight to see if she will admit to anything that she may have felt or seen that night? I can make an excuse that I need to borrow a textbook from her."

"What...?" Anna said with a screwed-up face.

"I'm positive she knows more than what she's willing to tell Mark. I think if I ask her alone, she will answer me more. I swear, I won't tell her anything about what we're doing, or anything about what happened to you. I'll just make out that I felt something to see if she'll own up to anything."

"For what it's worth, Anna, I think it's a good idea, the more info we can get, the better." Abbey chimed in.

Anna took in a deep breath and exhaled slowly. "Uhhh, okay. I guess you have a point. But just don't let her control the conversation and turn it into the Spanish Inquisition about us."

"Babe, I've got you." Boston said while walking over and delicately kissing her on the side of her neck. Boston quickly sent Brianna a text.

"Hey B! 4got my history txtbk & I need to study. Mind if I quickly pop over and borrow urs? I can get it bck 2 u 2morrow?"

"4 sure! Home now, come on over."

"OK! Brianna bought it. I'm gonna head over there now while she's home," Boston leaned down and kissed Anna goodbye before leaving her bedroom. Anna tingled at his touch.

"Ohh... come and look at this," Anna motioned Abbey over to her computer screen. "This web page is dedicated to Pennsylvania haunts. It's got like different postings, articles, pictures, video links, etc. Anyway, most of the info is about Gettysburg, but there are a couple of postings here about the Mack house. Look here," she pointed to an article titled—

Abbey cut her off by reading the article's first line, *"Infamous for being the birthplace of the now children's nursery rhyme, 'Mack House' is a legend in its own right for a much darker reason."* "That's a really exciting find, Anna!" she exclaimed as she continued to read aloud to herself. "Wow!" she said in amazement.

"The article reads almost exactly like my first encounter." Anna couldn't believe what she had just read. "Everything is the same except for her speaking to me. But the atmosphere, the physical impact, and the rest of it is the same."

"Who wrote the article? Maybe you could contact them?" asked Abbey hopefully.

"Well, I clicked on the author's profile. Her name is Sarah Baxter... says she lives in California. It gives me the option to email her, or there's also a link to her Twitter account... I could post something there too?" Before Abbey had a chance to reply, Anna decided to click on the small envelope icon that opened a pre-populated email to Sarah. "I can just start off light and send her a quick note to say that I enjoyed reading her post. Who knows if she'll respond, but it's worth a try, hey?"

"Why not? You should also just say that you had a similar experience at the Mack House and that you would like to ask her a couple of questions. That way she might be more open to replying if you were nice about her article and you're being polite, or at the very least, curious," Abbey suggested supportively.

"Good idea! There. Sent," Anna confirmed as she finished typing her quick message. Anna felt like she was on the right track.

"Wonder how long it will be before Boston will call to tell me how his conversation with Miss Wonderful went?" Anna snickered. "That was mean of me. But I tried to give her a chance once before, and she's always been so mean and sneaky."

"Brianna doesn't give us any reason to think she will change and suddenly be nice and act accepting toward you," Abbey noted worthily.

"Who knows? Maybe one day when she's older... people can change, I guess." Anna shrugged her shoulders. Anna beamed as her mind went back to the night before, and she pictured her and Boston dancing together. Abbey giggled as she looked at Anna.

"Let me guess, you're daydreaming about your man!" she jested.

Anna raised one eyebrow. "Something like that," she laughed as she pursed her lips. "Okay, let's go downstairs and get a tea and some of those sandwiches. I just love the Chai Tea Latte from the Keurig machine, it is de-licious!!"

"Yummm... that sounds good," Abbey replied excitedly.

"I'll have to excuse Boston, since Mom was making enough sandwiches for him. I'll just say that he had to go home for something. You know how excited Mom gets about feeding people, LOL."

Anna sat shaking her foot, not so patiently waiting for Boston to call. Not only was she anxious to hear how things went with Brianna, but it was Saturday and they were supposed to go out to dinner later that night. Finally, her cell phone buzzed with a text message from Boston.

"Pick u up @ 7? I want to surprise u with a romantic dinner. I'm not a tru romantic, but now & again..."

"Looking fwd to it! C U then xx"

"Wow, you look stunning!" Boston said as Anna opened her front door, wearing skinny jeans, a V-neck black lace button-down shirt with a white silk collar and white silk cuffs, patent leather black stiletto pumps with powder blue soles, and her black leather jacket. Anna decided to make a little extra effort, since Boston picked a romantic restaurant. Wearing her curly hair half up with a little knot at the top and a couple of tendrils hanging down each side of her face, Anna had finished off her look with a light pink plumping lip gloss. Anna wanted to wear something a little sexier than her usual more casual look for her mystery date night with Boston.

"Thanks," she smiled shyly. "Let's go," she added and closed the door behind her. "So, where are we having dinner?"

"Ciao Bella... if that's okay with you?"

"Awesome... that sounds really nice." Anna grinned with excitement. Ciao Bella was one of the most expensive and upscale restaurants in Cannon Falls. Anna hadn't been taken there on a date before. *Boston's breaking out the big bucks!* she jested to herself. "So how did the convo with Brianna go? Did you manage to squeeze any details out of her?" she asked skeptically.

"Actually, I did get a little. Bri admitted she could smell the perfume and she knew it wasn't yours. The whole thing really freaked her out. She also admitted that she swore to Mark that she is never going back there."

"Huh... so she admitted that she knows Mary is still there? That the old place really was haunted?"

"Yep... pretty much. So now you know that she smelled the perfume, you can stop contemplating if that piece of the night really happened," Boston confirmed as he gave her hand a gentle squeeze.

"Yep, I'm hoping I hear back from that woman I emailed. I just need to pull up my big girl socks and go back to Mary's house. Hopefully, Mary will speak to me again so I can figure out how to help her." Anna gently chewed on her lip as her nerves kicked in. "God... I can't believe I am seriously saying this stuff... it's insane!" she exclaimed.

"I'll give you that. I never thought that I or anyone else I know would be dealing with something like this. But I guess you hear stories of people going through all different types of paranormal experiences all the time. We'll just have to see if anything happens when you go back," Boston shrugged.

As they pulled the car up to Ciao Bella's parking lot, a few light raindrops began to fall. The brightly lit Italian villa building was filled with people bustling around inside. Some leaving, others arriving, and everyone dressed a little more formally than you see at most of the local eats. White lights lined the terracotta rooftop, and a few tall juniper trees edged the sides of the building. Anna could smell the olive oil and fresh garlic bread baking, which was a favorite appetizer for most guests. Ciao Bella was famous for their garlic bread alone.

"I swear it's nearly impossible to find a parking spot here on Saturday night, crazy busy!" Boston said as he finally pulled his car into a parking space and put it in park. He leaned over and began kissing Anna softly. The butterflies in her stomach buzzed around as they kissed for what seemed like an hour. Anna could feel the warmth spread across her whole body. Boston followed the deep kiss with a few subsequent pecks on her lips. "Hmm... god, I just love your soft lips," Boston said while slowly pulling away.

"I really like you kissing you too," she gently shivered.

"I feel like I'm going to just explode around you," he laughed as his eyes burned into hers.

"I know what you mean," she answered back.

"Come on… let's go eat. Don't want us to miss our reservation time. Even though I love the idea of staying here and kissing you for a while longer," he laughed.

"I am quite hungry… you know me and my appetite!" Anna said while opening her door.

"So how do you like your lasagna?" Boston inquired while shoving another massive forkful of shrimp linguine into his mouth.

"It is freakin' delicious!" she replied while rolling her eyes at him. "I was thinking, I don't know if you have anything going on tomorrow, but if you're free, maybe we could take a trip to the Mack House? Just for 30 minutes? I want to see if I get any feelings, vibes, or anything else."

"Of course, I can do that," Boston nodded. "I think it's good not to beat around the bush, and now that you know you want to move forward with this, you may as well figure it out sooner rather than later. You never know, maybe you won't hear or see anything."

The Mack House was open to the public on the weekends till five o'clock, so a couple of members from the Historical Society were working at the house. "True. Anyway, what do you want to do after we finish eating?" Anna asked, changing the conversation. The idea of going back to the Mack House still made her stomach hurt a little, but she knew that it would be the right thing to do.

"We don't have to, and I know this is a little bit of a surprise, but I would really like to take you to my house to meet my parents. They're home tonight for a change. Typically, they are out on Friday and Saturday nights with their friends or attending some function. Would that be okay with you?" Boston asked a little sheepishly.

Anna felt herself gulp. *Holy crap... meeting the parents already— no pressure, Anna!* she thought to herself. "Sssure, I would love that. That sounds nice," she replied nervously, her eyes a little wider than normal.

"Awww, babe, don't be nervous... they'll love you. I promise. We can do it another night if you prefer?" he asked supportively, adoring her at the same time as he watched her cheeks lightly flush.

"No, I want to meet them. Let's go tonight."

"Cool, they are literally out all the time for work stuff or whatever, so I wanted to seize the day and all that while they're home. I'll text Dad and let him know we'll be heading over within an hour."

"Perfect!" Anna replied excitedly. *Oh lord, I hope they like me. I hope I like them!* she pondered.

Anna's heart raced as they approached Boston's house. Her mind rattled off several situations of how his mom or dad would act toward her and how she would react to said situations. She also thought of various conversation topics she could discuss with them so they would have plenty to talk about. Boston pulled up to the impressive, large three-story brick home and parked just outside the three-car garage. As the double doors opened, Anna could see a black 2020 Ford F-150 Limited and what appeared to be a brand new large, white and very fancy Mercedes sedan sitting inside.

"Anna, it's wonderful to meet you finally!" exclaimed Peggy, Boston's mom, as they walked in the interior door from the garage. His parents were both sitting on a couple of cozy armchairs near the stone fireplace in their very spacious kitchen. As his parents walked over to greet them, his mom said to Anna, "You and football are the only two things Boston talks about these days," as she gently nudged Boston. This warmed Anna's heart as she felt it temporarily race.

Phew, this isn't so hard, Anna reassured herself. Anna's creative mind pictured meeting a mom who doesn't want to let any girl steal her son away... she always did have a good imagination. Anna admitted that maybe she had watched one too many afternoon thriller movies.

"Anna, as Peggy has pointed out, we've heard a lot about you. So how is your school year going? I imagine that you are already planning out what you will do after graduation. I know I started doing that my sophomore year. I was ready to break out by the end of Senior year," he giggled to himself.

"Oh yeah! I am thinking about going into architecture and interior design, so I have a couple of schools in mind. Possibly the

University of Gettysburg or Penn State, if I decide I want to venture a little further out. But I'm really close with my parents, so I need to give it some more thought." Anna smiled as she saw how his parents' faces lit up when they heard her mention her relationship with her mom and dad, which was all very true.

Anna spent the next couple of hours chatting away to his parents and helped his mom make some orange hot chocolates to complement the chilly fall night. The sight of Boston and his dad sitting in brown leather chairs in front of the large stone fireplace in the living room made Anna feel warm and very satisfied inside. Anna was over the moon that she seemed to get along really well with his parents. As she stood watching Boston, Anna suddenly caught Boston's eyes staring back at her. He gave her his wonderful cheeky grin. The moment sparked a flashback from that day in history class when Boston gave her that cheeky grin and asked her out after class. *Feels like we've been together for much longer than four weeks*, she sighed to herself.

"Anna, are you ready to go? It's getting close to your curfew," asked Boston sweetly.

"Gosh, I didn't realize the time! Sounds good," she replied.

"Well, Anna, it was really great to meet you," Peggy said while giving Anna a big hug goodbye.

"It was really great to meet you both, too!" Anna beamed back.

"Well, I'm sure we'll see you again soon... maybe for dinner next time?" asked Boston's dad, Tom. Anna looked at Boston for direction.

"Sure! Anna, would Wednesday night work for you? I don't have practice that night," Boston suggested.

"That would be great!" she exclaimed.

Anna didn't want her night to end as Boston drove her home. The car was warm and cozy, and music played quietly in the background. There was a certain sense of sadness that she couldn't shake. If she made all the rules, Boston would come inside her house, and they would stay up all night watching movies and talking and just cuddling together.

"What time should I come over tomorrow?" Boston asked, putting his car in park.

"Hmmm... how about eleven o'clock?" Anna found it hard to concentrate on anything other than the fact that she knew it was time to say goodnight to him, which meant she would get to steal his lips for a few moments longer.

"Cool, I'll see you the—" before he could finish his thought, Anna had locked onto his lips, kissing him more passionately than she ever had before, with a spontaneous burst of empowerment.

Eek... hope I'm not being too aggressive, she thought suddenly to herself. But given the fact that she could hear Boston let out a deep, whispering groan while kissing equally as intensively back, she was none too worried.

With one hand placed on his left cheek bone and the other rubbing the back of his head, Anna didn't want to let go. Boston intertwined his fingers locking them around her long curls; it felt so good to feel his hands on her. "Mmm..." Boston pulled back breathlessly. "I've got to stop, otherwise I'm not going to be able to let you out of my car," he smiled while licking his lips.

"Maybe I don't want you to let me go," Anna pouted.

"I'm never gonna really let you go, just temporarily so I don't implode. Self-preservation and all that," he laughed.

"That's probably the right thing to do," Anna tutted. "Goodnight Boston, I wouldn't want to be responsible for your imploding," she giggled, planting one last soft kiss on his lips.

"Goodnight, babe. See you tomorrow. I'll text you before bed." With that, Anna jumped out of his car and ran to her front door. The night air was very sharp and brisk. After making sure that Anna got inside, he drove away.

CHAPTER THIRTEEN

"It's still here," Boston said while reaching down under the Mack House steps and pulling out the front door key. The sun shone brightly and reflected off the warped windows, forcing Anna to squint. Boston opened the front door after giving it a good push. As they walked into the house, gray thick clouds began to roll in. Suddenly, the front door slammed shut behind Boston. "Jeez! That made me jump," he exclaimed.

Anna approached the aged and stained oval mirror, which was placed above a small half-moon table. As she stood facing the mirror, the face staring back at her changed from her own to someone else's. It was Mary. Anna jumped back but couldn't stop looking. Mary's mouth opened, forming words that Anna couldn't interpret. Tears ran down Mary's face as she abruptly began rapidly aging from looking like a young woman to an old lady with white hair. "Oh my god! Boston!" Anna screamed as she turned her head away and searched for him.

Suddenly, Anna sat up in bed breathing heavily, realizing that it was just a dream. *Oh my god, that was a freakin' weird ass dream,* she thought to herself. Then she focused her attention on something more positive, thinking about the amazing date she had with Boston the night before. Smiling, she pulled back her covers and jumped out of bed to go tell her mom, then to call Abbey and her friends to them all about her amazing date night.

"I feel really weird about going there today, but it's something that I have to do," Anna said while nibbling on her index finger and talking to Abbey on her phone.

"You'll be fine, just say 'eff it'!" Abbey cheered. "What time is the B-man coming over? I still can't believe you've met his parents already. I think someone's got it pretty ba-aaad!" Abbey squealed down the phone trying to lighten Anna's mood.

"You're a dork! He'll be here in about fifteen minutes. He's bringing me a caramel macchiato from Starbucks as a treat," she smiled.

"Awww, very nice! I'll just be babysitting Aubrey 'cause my mom's going over to my aunt's house. So call me if anything happens, okay? In fact, I'll be expecting a call but will take a text at the very least when you leave there," Abbey demanded.

"Yes ma'am. Well, you and Aubrey have fun hanging out," Anna laughed.

"Oh, don't you know it!" Aubrey is Abbey's nine-year-old going on thirteen-year-old little sister, and although they have a seven-year age gap, Abbey absolutely adores Aubrey, and they spend a lot of time together. Abbey signed up to get paid to babysit Aubrey, which is fairly often because both of her parents work at the local hospital; her mom is a doctor and her dad is the hospital administrator.

Suck it up Anna... just say 'eff it,' Anna convinced herself when she got butterflies thinking about Mary in her weird ass dream. Abbey and Anna had a mantra that they say anytime they must do something that makes them uncomfortable or nervous such as delivering a speech at school, auditioning for a play, and so on. They just say to themselves, "eff it!" and this meant don't worry about it, just get on with it and do your best. Basically, don't be a wuss and just go for it. Anna intended on casually walking around the house to see if she would hear, see, or sense anything at all.

"Hey Boston, how are you? Great game Friday, you're having a heck of a season!"

"Ah, thanks Mr. Ipswich. Well, it couldn't have come at a better time being my senior year and all. My parents and I are waiting to hear about some scholarships. They would prefer Penn State for obvious reasons."

"That's great! I know what they mean. We're also hoping that Anna doesn't stray too far," Anna's dad scoffed. Anna's dad was hoping that she goes to a school within driving distance and not somewhere far, like the West Coast. "Not sure what I am going to do without my architecture assistant here to help me. That reminds me, I need Anna to pick up some plans on Monday for the Marx's property from City Hall after school," he smiled proudly. "Well, Anna's in the kitchen with her mom, if you want to go through," her dad said while putting the leashes on the dogs. "Gotta take these crazy little buggers for a walk," he laughed.

"Oh, great, enjoy your walk," Boston said while heading into the kitchen. Anna was rumbling around in the fridge, looking for a bottle of water. As she closed the door, she saw Boston just standing there quietly.

"Argh! Boston! You nearly gave me a heart attack, you creep" Anna giggled as Boston slipped his arms around her waist.

"Hah! I couldn't resist the opportunity. It was literally staring me in the face," he said while planting a light kiss on her lips. "Are you ready to head out soon?"

"Yep, let me just go grab my jacket. Mom, we're getting ready to leave," Anna called nervously to her mom, who was busy in the walk-in pantry.

Her mom peeked her head out as she threw a few more items into a large black trash bag hanging on the handle of the door outside the pantry. "Oh, hi there Boston! Just doing some light purging," she gestured. "Okay, darling, you kids behave yourselves," her mom smiled.

"Okay, let's get this over with. Abbey was going to meet us, but she has to go to her aunt's house," Anna said as she came back into the kitchen after grabbing her jacket.

"Gotcha. Hey, I heard that she and Justin went out the other night again. He's pretty into her, you know."

"Hmmm. Abbey said that she had fun hanging out with him. I think she really likes him too. Look at us. We're quite the matchmakers," snorted Anna as they walked out of her front door.

As Anna and Boston pulled up to the Mack House, there were two other cars parked in the lot. The day was a perfect November day; a brisk, light wind blew around but there wasn't a cloud in the sky. A member of the Historical Society wearing a bright red coat stood outside by the front door handing out leaflets to people as they walked in. A box for collected donations sat nearby on a small table.

When Anna and Boston approached the front steps, the woman passed them the advertisement. "Thanksgiving Ball is only a week away. You can purchase your tickets inside, on our website, or at City Hall. Proceeds go to completing some of the much-needed maintenance work for the house," the blonde-haired woman with rosy cheeks said in a bubbly tone. Her gold leaf earrings dangled from her curly hair. "You two would make quite the couple at the ball," she smiled.

"Thanks so much!" Anna replied. For some reason, the woman's friendliness calmed her nerves.

"My parents will be going to this. They're co-sponsors for the event," Boston said while opening the front door for Anna.

"Oh cool!" Anna replied while stepping into the house.

"Any excuse for my mom to get dressed up in one of her fancy gowns," laughed Boston.

Boston went over to the man sitting at a small desk and paid the $5 entrance fees for himself and Anna, while Anna started to walk around the living room. "Feel anything?" Boston asked as he approached her.

"Nope... not yet. Let's go in the bedroom."

"Wow, Anna! Are we moving too quickly?"

"Ha ha... in your dreams, dork!" Anna giggled. She appreciated Boston's efforts to lighten the mood.

"Ouch," Boston pouted playfully.

Anna walked over to the corner of Mary's bedroom near the window and just stood quietly, trying to open herself up to Mary. She stood there for a few minutes while Boston stood by the doorway watching her.

Anna inhaled deeply as she suddenly caught the scent of flowery perfume. She heard a couple of light footsteps come into the room. She turned around expecting to see Boston walking toward her or another visitor. But no one was there except for Boston, still standing in the same spot. "Huh? Did you just move or did someone else just come into the bedroom and leave?" inquired Anna.

"Nope... only me. No one else has even come close to this room. In fact, the other visitors have all just left. Why?"

"Do you smell a florally scent? Or did you hear footsteps, like heels on the floorboards?"

"No," Boston replied suspiciously.

"I can smell that flowery perfume again, and I heard—" Anna froze.

"You heard what?" Boston quizzed but Anna didn't answer. "Babe, you heard what?" he repeated, but Anna stood silent.

Anna could hear the whispering voice again. Anna freaked out inside, but she had to make sense of it all. She was suddenly overwhelmed with the wave of sadness that came over her, so deeply that she could feel tears prick her eyes. The feeling of devastation made her want to burst into tears. The whispering sounds went quiet, and the voice became clearer, fading in and out again like a bad phone connection.

"Help... help... me... help me," the voice begged, fading in and out.

"Mary?" Anna whispered. More words followed.

"Please help me?" the sobbing words came more clearly and uninterrupted this time.

"Mary, is that you?" Anna whispered back. The fear had left her, and she felt braver than ever.

"Yes. Please help," the quiet female voice begged.

"I will. I will help you. Tell me how?" Anna demanded. She couldn't believe what was happening. Boston stood in shock, just watching what was happening in disbelief. He couldn't hear Mary, so he was just trying to piece the conversation together from what he was hearing Anna say.

"Find him," Mary replied.

"You want me to find Benjamin?" asked Anna.

"Please. I don't know..." Mary's voice began fading out again.

Anna looked at Boston. "She wants me to find Benjamin Watts or find out what happened to him."

"Holy shit," Boston gasped.

"Mary, wait! I don't know how. Can you show me how to help you?" Anna pleaded.

"The box in the floor," Mary whispered.

"A box in the floor somewhere?"

"Bed—" Mary's voice was fading out again.

"Bed?" asked Anna.

"Be—" Mary was gone, and seconds later the flowery perfume odor disappeared. Anna looked around the room, and then her eyes turned back toward Boston. Anna felt weak at the knees, like she was going to either pass out or burst into tears.

Boston sighed as he walked over to her and put his arms around her. "It's okay. You're okay," he whispered gently while holding her face delicately and making eye contact with her.

"She was so s-a-d!" Anna said as she burst into tears and sobbed.

"Anna, it's okay. Don't cry, babe. You're killing me. It's okay. I promise we're going to help her. She knows that now," he comforted her. Anna wanted to stop crying, but she just couldn't stop.

Boston just stood there holding her, letting her cry it all out. Feeling her body shudder as she cried weighed heavily on him emotionally in a way that he couldn't quite figure out how to digest.

After a few minutes, she stopped herself and pulled away. Wiping her eyes and breathing deeply through her nose, she exclaimed, "Oh my gosh. I'm so sorry Boston. I'm normally not so much of a crybaby, but I just felt so overwhelmingly devastated for her. It's like I could feel her sadness, loneliness, and turmoil - her complete and utter heartbreak."

"It's okay, babe. Don't apologize. I get it" he said, taking her hand and leading her out of the bedroom.

"God, I must look like a red-faced devil," Anna laughed, thinking about her hot, puffy face and black running mascara.

"Ha! No, you don't. You look beautiful," Boston replied while giving her hand a gentle squeeze. "Let's get out of here. I don't think you're going to get any more out of our visit here today."

Once Anna got back into her car, she opened up the visor mirror to see the damage. "Sorry, but I just need to clean up my face." She smiled gently as she wiped away the black mascara streaks and applied some Chapstick. As emotionally drained as Anna felt, she was able to relax by wiping away the tear marks and cleaning herself up. "So, where do you want to go?" asked Anna.

"Ladies choice," he answered.

"Let's go to the diner. I could do with some chili cheese fries and a deluxe hot chocolate. I need some comfort food," Anna settled.

"The diner it is. I have to agree that some chili cheese fries sound awesome!"

Boston was really intrigued to hear the full conversation with Mary, but he figured it was best to wait till he got to the diner to ask her about it. He figured that she probably needed a few minutes to relax and calm down from everything that had happened. Boston flicked on the radio. "Chances" by Five for Fighting was playing on his favorite station.

"I love this song!" Anna announced as she very quietly sang along. They finally pulled up at the restaurant.

"I'm starving!" Boston said as he walked around the car and opened the passenger door for Anna. Once inside, they sat down in a booth toward the back of the diner where they had some privacy.

"God, did that really just happen?! It feels so surreal. In fact, I had a strange dream last night that we were at the house, and I could see Mary in a mirror. She aged like 60 years right in front of me within seconds. But the fact that I just had basically a conversation with her is bending my mind!" Anna shook her hands and lifted her head back.

"I know. It's hard to believe... When you were talking to her, I could obviously hear what you were saying, but you just looked shocked."

"I was. But the funny thing is, the more she spoke the less scared I felt. In fact, it was just the opposite."

"What did she say to you?" Boston shifted around in his seat in anticipation.

"It started off like before..." Anna paused as the waitress came over and placed their food and drinks on the table. Once the waitress was out of earshot, Anna continued, "It was like last time with the bad connection type thing and the whispering. But eventually her voice got clearer, and I could hear her. She was sobbing and begging me to help her find Benjamin. When I asked how, she told me about some box that is under the floorboards near her bed."

"Holy shit! I guess the box that she told you about must have something in it that's very important. We have to go find it!" Boston exclaimed.

"For sure, but if we are going to start digging up floorboards, it will have to be at night, and we'll need to get the right tools and supplies."

"Right. But we'll also need nails and stuff to lay the boards back down with. And, we are going to need help if we don't want to take all night to do this," Boston assured her.

"I'm thinking Abs and Jay will help me," Anna said hopefully.

"Cool. Let's go back one night this week then, once it's all been closed up and it's dark."

Anna sighed... "Ugh I just hope we don't get caught and that the key is still in the same place as it was before, so we can get in."

"It will work out! I could do Wednesday night after we eat dinner at my parents'. I'll just tell them that you have to be back early, so they don't spend all night after dinner talking." suggested Boston.

"That works. I'll talk to Abbey and Jay to make sure that day works for them - if they are willing to help, that is."

"Sounds like a plan. I can grab some of my dad's tools and whatnot. The guy seriously has a Home Depot in our garage!" laughed Boston.

"Ha! Your dad is super nice and funny," Anna giggled.

"Yeah, he's cool. So, are you glad you made the decision to go back to the Mack House? How do you feel about it now?" Boston asked on a more serious note.

"Still feel a bit weirded out, but I'm glad I went back. Knowing what I know now, I just want to help her more than ever because I've felt her pain."

CHAPTER FOURTEEN

The next morning, Anna left the house in a hurry. She had already spoken to Abbey the night before, and she was on board with the plan. In fact, Abbey could barely contain her excitement. Now she just had to get Jay to agree. Anna gave two beeps when she pulled up to Abbey's house. It took Abbey all of five seconds to come running out of her front door. "Wow, that was fast, Abs!"

"I was waiting for you to pull up," she beamed back.

"Would that excitement have a little something to do with Justin?" teased Anna.

"Maybe," she grinned. "But I can't wait for us to tell Jay what we are going to do on Wednesday!" Abbey said with her eyes widened. Anna couldn't help herself and laughed back at Mrs. Cool being so obvious. The two girls finally pulled up at Jay's house.

"Hey, girls!" Jay said as he jumped in the backseat. "How come you picked Abs first?" he asked, confused being that he lived closer to Anna's house.

"We had some girl-talk to do before I picked you up, so I thought I would spare you from it," Anna replied confidently. Jay just laughed.

"Jay... I really need your help with something. But it will be very risky, so I totally understand if you don't want to do it. I'm just asking you to keep this to yourself. You cannot tell anyone about it."

"Oh god, what is it? You're freaking me out with all the seriousness," Jay joked.

"Okay, just please keep an open mind"

"Jeez, just spit it out already, Anna!" Jay demanded, getting annoyed. Anna proceeded to tell him everything that had happened in the past few weeks with Mary and her plans for later that week.

"Woah. So firstly, holy shit, this is insane! And second, Jesus, Anna! You guys could get arrested for property damage, trespassing, and whatever else. Are you out of your minds? What if you get caught?!" he gasped.

"Ugh, grow up, Jay, and quit sounding like a freakin' baby," snorted Abbey.

"Shut up, Abs! Anna, seriously, are you really going to go through with this?" he asked anxiously.

"Yes, Jay, I am! And you know me well enough to know that I'm not lying about any of this. I am being 100% real, and I'm committed now to helping Mary," Anna yelled back defensively.

"Grrr... you're all insane! And I mean totally insane, risking getting put in juvie for something that six weeks ago you hardly knew anything about. I seriously can't believe that you are going to do this!" Jay said shaking his head in disbelief. "But... I can't stand by and not help my best friends when they need me. I want to know the complete breakdown of the details, though; how we are going to do this, who's bringing what—everything." Jay added as he slouched into the backseat.

"Yay, Jay!" Abbey celebrated by clapping.

"Seriously, Jay, you're the best. Thank you so much! I know what you are risking, and I truly appreciate it... it means a lot to me," Anna said affectionately.

"If you all are going to do something this crazy, you need 'this guy's' brain to help you do it," he joked while pointing both thumbs toward his own chest.

"Great! That's settled then," Abbey confirmed as Anna's car pulled up to the school parking lot. Justin stood waiting at the top of the steps leading to the school's entrance with Boston.

"Damn, Abs looks sexy today!" Justin commented to Boston as Abbey approached from the parking lot toward the steps wearing black leggings, a cream lightweight sweater, black and white shearling bomber jacket, and some black Sorrel strap boots. Her large gray leather tote bag hung over her shoulder, which had blonde curls cascading down on it.

"You still thinking about asking her to the Winter Ball next month?" asked Boston.

"Yeah... think she'll go with me?"

"From what I've heard from Anna, I'm pretty sure she will," Boston confirmed.

"Cool! I'll ask her now then," Justin beamed.

"Hey Justin!" Abbey smiled confidently. She could tell that Justin was watching her like a hawk the entire length of the parking lot.

"Hey Abs... you look great. Nice outfit."

"Hey," Boston greeted Anna as he leaned in and kissed her a little longer than Anna expected.

"Let's get inside, you're freezing cold," Boston said gently.

"Awww... you're so thoughtful!" Anna jested as she tickled his waist through his coat.

"Hey... whoa, that tickles," Boston laughed as he twisted to get away from Anna's grip.

God, I wish I could just hang out with Boston all day, Anna thought to herself as she walked through the school's front door. Abbey and Justin hung back and followed slowly behind.

The school lunch bell chimed, and Abbey came bursting out of her classroom doors and hurried along the hallway to meet Anna. "Oh my god, Anna, I have to talk to you!" Abbey shrieked.

Anna whirled around in the hallway to face Abbey as she was walking up from behind. "What? What's going on, Abs?" Anna replied as they walked toward to the lunchroom cafeteria.

Justin asked me this morning to go with him to the Winter Ball!" Abbey celebrated.

"Yay! Abs, that's awesome! When did he ask you?"

"In class today. It was super sweet. He passed me a little folded handwritten note in class that said, 'Abs will go to the Winter Ball with Justin' and a checkbox next to a 'Yes' and a 'No.' Obviously I checked the 'Yes' box and passed it back to him," she replied excitedly.

"Awww, my god, that's supes adorable, Abs! I'm so happy for you. OMG, we can all go together because Boston and I are going together too."

"Yay, that will be super fun!" exclaimed Abbey. "Well let's go see where Jay is sitting. We need to see if he is planning on asking Becky. It would be nice if we could all go together," she added.

"I'm sure he will," Anna said while grabbing a tray, "Seems like he and Becky are getting along really well. They've gone on a ton of dates together."

That night, Anna tossed around the idea of telling her mom about what had happened at the Mack House on Sunday and on the night that she and Abbey had a weird encounter outside the house. Anna was hesitant, though. Her mom might think that either Anna was letting her imagination run wild, or she would be super mad because she had told Anna not to go back there. Anna was also concerned that it might complicate things and make her mom worry.

Anna wouldn't dream of telling her about what the group plans to do on Wednesday night. But she couldn't help that a small part of her didn't like keeping things from her mom—it made her feel super guilty. But Anna had to do what she had to do. This was about helping Mary and not about herself. Just then, her phone vibrated. She looked down to see a text from Boston.

"*Shud I ask Justin to help us Wed night?*"

"*Ummm, no thx. Please don't tell him!*"

"*He won't tell anyone. I promise x*"

"*I know. But I wud prefer him not 2 b involved xx*" *The less people know about this the better,* Anna thought to herself.

"*Ok See u 2morrow :) xx*"

"*Thx :) xxx*"

God, I can't wait to see her tomorrow, Boston thought to himself as he read Anna's last text message. He flicked through Netflix while lying in his bedroom, but he could barely think about watching TV. Boston was well and truly crazy about Anna. He contemplated driving over to her house and throwing candy at her bedroom window but figured he would get caught by his parents in trying to leave his house or get caught by her mom or dad standing outside their house. Either way would definitely not be a good situation. So, instead, he drifted off to sleep.

The following day at school, Anna, Abbey, Jay, and Boston decided to meet by the school bleachers during lunch to talk about their plans for Wednesday night. Anna and Jay headed down the hallway after coming out of art class together. "Do you mind if we go somewhere to get lunch? I didn't bring any, and I really don't want to eat anything from the cafeteria," Jay said sheepishly.

"Ugh, Jay, we're supposed to be meeting everyone at the bleachers. Let me call Boston, and you call Abbey. Tell her to meet us at my car, you nerd," Anna said in annoyance.

"Sorry Anna," Jay pouted.

"It's fine, I just hope neither of them have already started walking over to the football field. I'm sure they wouldn't have made it too far," she reassured him. Luckily, Jay and Anna caught the others in time, and they headed out of the parking lot. Their first stop was 'the strip,' one of Cannon Falls' main roads lined with many fast-food restaurants, gas stations, and such.

"Number 5 large size with a Dr. Pepper and an extra burger please. Number 2 without mayo and a Diet Coke, plain grilled chicken sandwich—just the sandwich—and a number 4 with 2 chicken strips and a lemonade. Anything else, guys?" asked Anna as she sat by the Burger Cannon drive-thru menu.

"Actually, I'll make mine a large Dr. Pepper," added Jay.

"Seriously, Jay, where are you going to put all that?" scoffed Abbey.

"That will be 24 dollars and 75 cents please," announced the cashier through the speaker.

"Here, Boston, I'll get it," confirmed Jay as Boston began to dig into his pockets.

"Ah, thanks, man!" Boston replied. Anna thought it was rather cute that Jay was being so nice to Boston. She was hoping that they would become friends, since Jay was the closest thing to a brother that Anna had.

The foursome sat in Anna's car in the parking lot back at school while eating their lunch and strategizing on how to execute their plan for the Mack House on Wednesday. "So how many crowbars and hammers does your dad have, Boston?" asked Jay.

"Trust me, he definitely has enough for all of us, and plenty of nails too. We should be good as far as tools go," he confirmed.

"How are we going to get in again without breaking in?" Abbey asked.

"There's a key under the front doorsteps that should still be there from a few weeks ago when Mark used it to get us in," assured Anna.

"What about flashlights? We'll need those or lanterns... it would be a bad idea to have a big flood light glowing up the place like Christmas," Jay jested.

"No doubt. My dad's got a few flashlights and lanterns; I'll bring those too," Boston said while sucking on his straw.

"Excellent! Can't think of anything else we would need... I mean, some invisible cloaks would be cool!" laughed Jay.

"When we get there, I will try to get some more specific answers from Mary, so we don't spend our time digging up half the bedroom floor unnecessarily," Anna added. "If I can, that is."

"Um-hum. What time are you picking us up, Anna?" Abbey nodded.

"How about 7:30? I'll pick you up after we eat dinner with Boston's parents."

"I'll pick you up from your house, Anna, for dinner," interrupted Boston. "I would rather us go there in my car. That way, if someone does see a car parked outside of the Mack House on Wednesday night, it will be mine they see and not Anna's."

Protective, Anna comprehended as she caught Abbey flash her a smile in the rear-view mirror. Anna knew that Abbey was thinking the exact same thing. *How cute, that he's so protective of me*, she smiled to herself.

Later that night, as Anna sat thinking through the events to come the following day, she felt mainly anxious about getting caught by someone but also kind of excited to begin her journey in solving the heart-torn mystery of Benjamin Watts for Mary. She decided to give Boston a call so she could speak to him before bed. "Boston, are you sure you want to do this tomorrow? I just keep thinking about what Jay said the other day. We could get arrested and end up in juvie, and it would be all my fault and—."

"Calm down, babe. I know how important this is to you and to Mary. I want to help her too—we all do. There is no way I would let you do this alone," Boston interrupted.

"Boston, you just blow my mind sometimes. I really appreciate you saying that and doing this with me. It really means a lot to me. I can't thank you enough," Anna said, trying to temper the unbelievable feeling of happiness that almost brought a tear to her eye.

"Anna, you have no idea how much you mean to me. I will always have your back. Arghh, god, I just wish I could see you now!" Boston said in frustration.

"I know what you mean. Are you still coming over on Saturday night?" inquired Anna.

"Yep! So, you said your parents are going to the Thanksgiving Ball at City Hall, right?"

"They are... actually, I guess they will see your parents there, right?"

"They should... that's cool," replied Boston.

"It will give them a chance to hang out a little while and talk about us," laughed Anna. "I was thinking we could just order pizza or Chinese and rent a movie or watch Netflix?" Anna suggested.

"Sounds great! Get some quality time in with my girl," Boston boasted.

CHAPTER FIFTEEN

Wednesday finally arrived and Anna was feeling anxious about the mission they were about to embark on later that night. "I must say, I feel very CIA or MI6 or whatever... it's like we're on CSI Cannon Falls," shrilled Abbey as they passed Jay in the school hallway and gave him a knowing nod.

"Ha ha, you're such a dork! But I know how you feel. I hope to God that we don't get caught... otherwise we're screwed – like, big time!' Anna said cautiously.

"Oh, we'll be fine, Anna. Don't worry. I firmly believe that when you do something for the right reasons, things will turn out okay," Abbey assured her.

Jay crept up behind Anna as she stood switching out her textbooks in her locker. "You're sure you want to go through with this?" Jay said in his best serial killer voice. Anna gasped.

"Ugh, seriously, Jay! Not the best day to be sneaking up on

me!" Anna snapped, unamused.

"Oh, take a chill pill. You're fine... I'm sorry," Jay said in his goofy Roger Rabbit voice, as he shrugged his shoulders up to his ears.

"Ha! Seriously, you're still doing that!" Anna giggled. The look on Jay's face was rather dopey, which made it impossible for her to stay mad at him.

"Anyway, yes, I'm still 100% positive that I want to go through with this. Are you?"

"Wouldn't miss it for the world!"

Just then, Anna felt her phone vibrate as she looked down to see a text message from Boston pop up.

"Pick u up at 5 for dinner?"

Anna frantically messaged back before walking into her English Lit class. Mr. Woodrow has a zero-cell phone policy in his classroom. If you're caught with it in your hand, it goes in his desk drawer until class is over.

"Sounds good x"

"Cool! xx"

"Dinner was amazing, and your mom is a great cook! What was that dish called again?" Anna asked while changing out of a dressy sweater and throwing on an oversized old black hoodie over her white tank top.

"Beef goulash, it's my favorite. Actually, I asked her to make it, so you could try it," said Boston, feeling pretty proud of himself. Boston drove carefully along the dimly lit 106 road, doing his best to ignore the distraction of Anna changing her sweater right next to him. The plan was for Anna and Boston to get Jay from his house first, before picking Abbey up from hers and heading to the Mack House.

"Awww, how sweet," Anna beamed as she entwined her fingers with his.

As Boston's car drove past the Mack House as they headed toward Anna's subdivision, Anna glanced at the dark old building that stood silent in the cold November night. Anna inhaled quickly.

"Are you nervous, babe?" Boston could hear her breathing change.

"Not so much about Mary. But I'll be glad when this is over—once we've found the box and everyone is home without getting arrested."

"I get it—but seriously, try not to worry too much. We'll be fine," he assured her, grabbing her hand and squeezing it tightly.

"I'm sure you're right."

After picking up Jay and Abbey, the foursome arrived at Mary's House. "Ooh god, it looks super creepy in the dark!" Abbey shuddered.

"I must say, I've never had any interest in coming here, but I get the ghost story theme that appeals to some peeps," Jay agreed. "Ohhh m-a-n!"

"What is it, Jay?" asked Anna.

"I left my Ghostbusters proton pack at home." He burst into a fit of laughter.

"Don't be an ass, Jay," demanded Abbey.

"Oh, come on... I'm just trying to shed a little humor on the situation," he laughed.

"Okay, we're here! You guys grab the lanterns and flashlights, and I'll grab the tool bag," ordered Boston as he turned the car off. There was a certain dead silence that filled the air around the house. The only sound came from the dried leaves blowing off the trees and hitting the pavement and the creaking of the tree limbs swaying in the night breeze.

"This place is seriously eerie," Boston muttered to himself quietly.

"It is, let's get on with it. Abbey, can you shine your flashlight by the stairs here while I try and fish out the front door key from beneath them?" directed Anna.

"Wow! Seriously?! That's the famous hiding place? Talk about obvious," Abbey scoffed.

"I know, right! But it's worked well so far, I guess," smiled Anna. Anna reached her hand around the small hole under the stairs. "What the heck?" she said while scrambling her arm around in search of the key. "Abbey, can you shine the light in here a little closer," she said in frustration. "Ugh, WTF, it's not here!" she screamed under her breath.

Boston walked over to where Anna was searching. "Watch out—I'll take a look," he said.

"It's not here, Boston, I don't understand."

"I'm sure it's here somewhere, Anna." He searched for a few more moments longer and gave up. "Huh, it's really not here."

"Argh, that's just fantastic!" Anna snorted.

"Well, maybe we can find another way in?" Jay walked up to the front door and tried turning the knob, just in case on the off chance someone had forgot to lock the old place up.

"I know, I'll just phase myself inside—ugh!" Anna huffed.

"Without breaking and entering, I don't think there is another way," Abbey turned her flashlight off.

"Let's just go and come back another night when we have a game plan for breaking in," Anna suggested. "Sorry, Mary," she shrugged.

"Anna's right, let's just go guys," Boston agreed.

Anna walked up to the Mack House and put her hand on the front door. "We'll be back, Mary. I hope you can hear me," Anna turned around and began walking down the front steps toward the parking lot.

Suddenly, Anna heard a clicking noise like a bolt moving. She turned sharply to face the front door again. "NO W-A-Y," she whispered to herself. Anna took a couple of steps back toward the house and placed her hand on the doorknob.

"Anna, come on—it's okay, we can come back," Boston shouted from the parking lot.

"Just hang on a sec. Can you come here please?" she replied.

"OK," he surrendered.

As Boston approached Anna, she twisted the knob and it turned. "I think she just unlocked it!" she said in amazement.

"Watch out, I'll give it a little shove—I remember it was sticky last time. We'll see what happens." With that, Boston twisted the knob and pushed on the door. Miraculously, it opened. "Holy crap!" he exclaimed. "I can't freakin' believe this!"

"She unlocked the door for us," Anna said quietly, shaking her head in disbelief.

"I swear the handle wouldn't turn when I tried before," Jay confirmed. "How is this possible?"

"How do you think? It was Mary—" Abbey was almost speechless for the first time in the last 10 years.

Inside the home, the group made their way to Mary's bedroom. "Come on, let's get moving." Boston led the group into the house as they turned on their lanterns and flashlights. "We don't have much more than a couple of hours till you have to be home, Anna," he added. "We need to start pulling up the floorboards from near the wall by her bed. I read online that it's the easiest way to start removing them. Jay, can you help me move the bed? If the box is supposed to be near her bed, it would be best to move the bed to the opposite side of the room," Boston said as he commandeered the box removal expedition.

"Sure, man!" Jay replied. "Abbey, can you take a look out the window and just make sure that there aren't any headlights coming our way?"

"Good idea. I'm starting to get a little paranoid that someone will drive by and see our lights inside the old place too." She gently pulled back the lace curtain to one side and checked both directions of 106 for cars. "We're good, but I'll keep my eye out," she confirmed.

Boston and Jay lifted the dark oak bed just barely above the floorboards and moved it over to the side of the bedroom by the door; the space itself wasn't very big.

"Hold on... let me just think for a minute. I just want to walk around where the bed stood to see if I get any vibes on where the box might be, exactly." Anna paced the space slowly, asking the question to Mary in her mind to give her a sign as to where the box would be hidden. The faded wooden floors creaked beneath her feet as she gently stroked the bridge of her nose with her index finger while concentrating hard. Her friends stood silent as they watched her in anticipation. "Alright, I think it's around this area where Mary stood the other day. So I'm thinking it's around here," she announced.

"Okay, let's get started by the corner of that side of the wall then," Boston suggested as he picked up a crowbar and crouched down by the corner by the wall. He began pulling on the crowbar to loosen the board, which lifted up after a couple of tugs. "It should get easier from now, since the first one's out," Boston smiled with a sense of self achievement, as he continued to pull up the second board. Anna walked over with her crowbar and began pulling up floorboards next to the ones that Boston had pulled up.

"Let's hope we find this box fairly quickly." Jay began pulling up boards behind the ones Anna pulled up.

Abbey walked across the room to where the others were crouching down. Suddenly she saw headlights in the distance out of the small window. "Guys there's a car coming! Turn off the lanterns, now!" she gasped. Luckily, the car turned off down another road before getting any closer to the Mack House. "Phew... it's turned off the road. I'll stay here and play lookout, make sure no one else comes along without us knowing," she suggested.

"Brilliant, Abs! Thanks," Anna responded.

The threesome had pulled up 15 floorboards, 5 across and 3 rows down with no sign of the box yet. "Ugh! I feel like we're just never going to find it. And we still have to put all these back down again." Anna ran her fingers through her hair in frustration.

"Calm down, babe. We've only been here like 30 minutes. We'll find it. Just be patient." Boston rubbed her shoulders.

"Right, but we don't have that much time tonight, and pretty soon, we're going to run out of floorboards on this side of the room. I really thought we would have found it by now. We're past where I thought it would be," she huffed.

"Ask Mary, Anna," suggested Abbey.

"That's the other thing. I haven't even felt her since we've been here. Even earlier I was trying to open my mind up to let her show me where it is, and nothing happened which is kind of strange."

"Well, you haven't tried to speak to her properly. Maybe your mind is too preoccupied," Abbey said, walking over to her. She could tell her friend was starting to get upset.

"I don't know. I just hope I haven't put you all at risk being here for us to find nothing and it all be a complete waste of time," she shrugged.

"Look, why don't we give you a minute to yourself?" asked Boston.

"Yeah, okay. Do you all mind stepping out into the other room and let me have a minute to see if I can contact her?" she requested. The group agreed and squeezed past the bed. Abbey gave her best friend's arm a little supportive grab as she walked past her and out of the room. "Thanks," Anna whispered.

Once everyone had passed through the door, Anna stood looking around the room, lit now only by one small lantern that sat on the floor by her feet. Mainly darkness surrounded her. Anna took a deep breath and calmed her mind, slowing her thoughts. She concentrated on communicating with Mary.

"Mary, are you here? Can you hear me?" She sat quietly waiting for a response, but there was nothing. Everything was silent. "Mary, please, I need you to help me," she added, but again there was no sound. Anna turned to face the window. "You have to help us. Please talk to me!" Anna begged.

Suddenly the flowery scent that had announced Mary's presence once before returned. Anna turned around to see Mary in her black dress standing near the bedroom armoire, elegantly and perfectly poised. She looked completely whole this time, like she was a living person, as opposed to having a more transparent appearance like she did before.

Anna felt overwhelmed about the vision in front of her. "Mary," was the only thing Anna could say at first.

"Anna," she replied.

"Mary, you must help us. I'm trying to find your trinket box, and we don't have much time," she pleaded, looking down at the floorboards they had already pried up. "Can you tell me exactly where it is?"

Mary nodded slowly, acknowledging Anna's request. She began to walk very slowly over to the opposite side of the room and pointed to some floorboards that had not yet been removed. Anna was still unclear as to the exact spot. Mary could see Anna's confusion. She pulled a white lace handkerchief out of the sleeve of her dress and threw it on the floor. She pointed to the where the handkerchief landed. Mary's face looked distressed still, but Anna realized that this was the first time that she couldn't hear her crying.

"Thank you, Mary, please don't be sad. We're going to find

out where Benjamin is and what happened to him. I promise you. We will do everything in our power to help you," Anna said with a gentle smile.

"A thousand thank-yous," Mary whispered as she faded away before Anna's eyes.

Anna summoned her friends back into the bedroom. "Guys—I've made progress!" she said, still shaking from the experience. Anna pointed to the ground where the handkerchief lay as the group re-entered the bedroom.

"Hmpfh, that wasn't there before?!" Boston said in disbelief. "But let's make this quick. Jay, can you give me a hand to pull up those couple of planks?" Boston asked as he picked up the small lace material and handed it to Anna.

The boys tugged and tugged on their crowbars pulling up the boards. Boston felt around the dirt below the cobweb-filled rafters. "Hey! I think I've got it! Wait, it's caught on something," he said, maneuvering the box around to free it. "Okay, I've got it!" he said, pulling the small wooden dust-covered box out of the space beneath the floorboards and passing it to Anna. "Here you go, babe. You should be the one to open it."

"Oh my god, I can't believe this," Anna said, amazed. Anna bent down, took it gently out of Boston's hands, and wiped the dust away.

"Huh, what's that on the top of it?" asked Abbey completely bemused by the whole ordeal.

"It's a silver nameplate," replied Anna.

"Well, what does it say?!" Abbey could barely contain herself.

"It just has the initials 'M. M.' engraved on it, Mary's initials, obviously." Anna carefully unhinged the small lock and opened the box very slowly.

"Man, I'm not gonna lie. This is pretty amazing," Jay commented as everybody stood in bewilderment by what they witnessed.

As the box opened, papers revealed themselves. "Guys! Lights out!" Abbey shouted as another car approached. "This one isn't turning, so it's going to drive right past us," Abbey confirmed.

"You know what, guys, I'm just as curious as you all, but we can't do this here right now. Let's get everything put back in its place. Then we can look through the box after we leave here," Boston said nervously.

"True. If we get caught, we may never know what's in there," Jay responded.

Once Abbey had given the all-clear, the group moved feverously, nailing the floorboards back into place. "Wow, that went fast!" Anna smiled as she hammered in the last nail.

Jay and Boston began moving the furniture back in the room, as Abbey and Anna pushed Mary's bed back into place. Boston unrolled the rug to conclude their adventure for the evening.

"Let's get the heck out of here! I'm leaving an anonymous note for the Historical Society about people using the hidden key. I'll leave it in the postbox. I don't want anyone else coming here on a ghost hunt and tormenting Mary anymore!"

"Or maybe we just need to check the next few days for it, and then you should keep it, Anna. That way you can get in whenever you want or need to speak to Mary?" suggested Jay.

"You know, Jay, every once in a while you do have some good ideas! I'm gonna do exactly that."

CHAPTER SIXTEEN

The group piled into Boston's Mustang and quickly departed from the Mack House parking lot. "Anna, where do you want to go to now? Where's the best place to check the box out?" Boston questioned.

"Um, I don't mind. I need to be home in 30 minutes, so somewhere not too far. I could sure use a white chocolate mocha though… it's bloody chilly tonight!"

"Yum! Yes, Starbucks is my vote too," Abbey pleaded in support.

"Fine with me," Jay added.

"Sounds like a plan! I'll go through the drive-thru though then pull into a parking spot. Then you can crack that box open in private," Boston grabbed Anna's hand and shot her that look that made her want to melt. Anna felt herself quiver as she smiled back at him.

"Let's see what you've got in here, Mary," Anna said while gently opening the small ebony-stained wooden box. Anna could almost hear everyone holding their breath in anticipation. "Here, Boston, hold these for a second," Anna gently handed over some documents that she pulled out of the box. "I can feel a couple of things at the bottom." Anna thought anxiously, *Please let there be something useful in here.*

"Woah, what is that?" asked Boston as she pulled gently on a small silver chain from the bottom of the box.

"It's an oval-shaped locket. It's got a heart inscribed on it," she said while holding the silver necklace up toward the car's interior light. Anna gently turned it around. "There's something else inscribed on it... 'To My Love,'" Anna read aloud. "Oh, poor Benjamin."

"Open it!" Abbey hurried her. As Anna moved the pendant down and held it over the wooden box, she slowly pulled it open by unclasping it.

"What is that?" Abbey asked in confusion when a wispy fluff nearly floated out.

"Weird," Jay added.

"It's a clipping of hair," Boston announced.

"It's a clipping of Benjamin's hair, I imagine," Anna confirmed. "I remember hearing about these in history class. Civil war soldiers would give these to their sweethearts before leaving for battle. It was supposed to comfort them in the event that they didn't make it back home."

"That is the saddest thing ever. I guess Mary refused to give up hope and instead wore this always," Abbey frowned.

"I think you're right," agreed Anna.

"What is the other thing at the bottom of that box?" inquired Jay. Anna pulled out a piece of blue silk ribbon. "Huh, I wonder why she was keeping this so safe," she asked.

"I don't know... could be a few different reasons, I guess. Maybe it was a gift from someone," Boston quizzed.

"Well, besides these papers, there is nothing else inside the box. Listen, it's getting late, and I know you probably think this is stupid, but I kinda want to just read through these documents by myself first. It's just in knowing how Mary feels—."

Abbey interrupted, "Anna you're not stupid for feeling that way. I think we can all understand that. You have a bond with Mary now; she chose you to help her. It's okay."

"Thanks, Abs. I will tell you guys about everything after I've gone through it all."

When Anna finally made it to her bedroom, she felt exhausted from the evening's big events. After placing the antique box on her desk, Anna changed into her favorite cozy fleece pajamas, washed her face, and climbed into bed with the intention of watching her favorite new show on Netflix to relax her brain. *I still can't believe what we did today. Mary looked so real, almost alive. Super weird!* She huffed. A familiar sound buzzed from her iPhone. Before looking to see who had texted her, Anna already knew.

"*Goodnight. Hope u sleep well dream of me and I'll c u 2morro xx :)*"

"*LOL I'll try. Thank u 4 2day!! BTW you looked very sexy with a crowbar ;) Sweet dreams xoxo.*"

Anna fell asleep almost as soon as her head hit the pillow.

Benjamin entered through the front door of the pretty quaint home and approached Mary as she stood peeling potatoes with a small knife. He handed her a very small package wrapped in brown paper with a white string tied around it. "What's this, my love?" she looked inquisitively at him and smiled sweetly. As Mary began to unravel the paper, a light powder-blue silk ribbon revealed itself

"For our wedding," Benjamin said. "Something blue," he smiled. Mary thrusted her arms around his neck and held onto him tightly. Fighting back the tears, a couple of drops escaped her. "I know I'm departing tomorrow to take my orders with my regiment, but I want to give you something to make you think happy thoughts. I cannot wait to make you my beautiful wife, Mary. I cannot wait till we can spend every day together for the rest of our lives, unless you would tire of me before that," he spoke softly into her hair.

Anna woke with tears streaming down her face. *It seemed too real to be a dream.* She thought to herself. Anna could literally feel Benjamin's anxiety of going to war and having to leave Mary. Although Anna was in a deep sleep, she couldn't shake the feeling that it was Benjamin who invited Anna into Mary's home to bear witness to such a sentimental moment between himself and Mary. Anna had been contemplating why the ribbon was in the box, and now she was convinced that Benjamin had just shown her. Anna decided she couldn't wait a moment longer to read through the documents from the box. There was no way she was going to be able to fall back asleep now.

Anna climbed out of bed, washed her hands in her en suite, switched on the table lamp on her desk, and sat down. Anna had read that the best way to handle old documents was to ensure that your hands were clean and dry. Gently opening the wooden box, she pulled out the first letter she found from its envelope. It was a letter from Benjamin, and from the looks of it, it was sent to Mary while he was in a battle. "Wow," she whispered to herself.

Anna could tell that it had been folded and unfolded a hundred times over. The many creases ran deep through the pages like veins. She was afraid that the letter would tear apart as she unfolded it as carefully and slowly as possible.

My darling Mary,
    I know these turbulent times weigh heavy on your heart, but I do hope that you are proud of me. I hope that you are proud of me

for protecting the Union States and aiding in the success of the war. I hope you are proud of me for protecting our home and the future and freedom of our unborn children. I miss you every day that I am away, and I am counting the days till I can see your face again and we can be married.

You are my heaven on this hell on earth. I will forever keep you safely in my dreams till I ride home. I love you forever

– Your Benjamin

Oh my god, poor Benjamin, poor Mary, Anna thought to herself, as tears pricked her eyes and fell one by one down her cheeks. The sadness she felt for the couple was overwhelming. At that moment, she also pondered what it would feel like if she and Boston were in their place. Her heart sank immediately, and tears pricked her eyes again. Anna wondered just how many times Mary would have read that letter either out of devastation or for comfort.

Anna took in a deep breath and let out a slow gasp in silence before grabbing her cell phone to check the time; it was 5:00 a.m., and Anna had the sudden urge to talk to Boston.

"Mornin sunshine! Want 2 meet me 4 brkfast?"

Knowing it would be a while before she heard back from him, she felt comforted by just communicating with him, which in turn made her feel closer to him in that moment. Anna returned to sifting through the papers. She came across more letters from Benjamin, an incomplete marriage license that made Anna wince, and some military documents including regimental orders. "This should help Mary," Anna said to herself.

The orders stated what regiment and class Benjamin was in as well as where he was to report for duty and on what date. Anna used her phone to take a photo of the orders document, remembering to turn off her flash just like in museums. This way she would always have the information on hand when doing her research. The deed to Mary's house was also in the box. Another letter was titled to Benjamin from Mary, which appeared to have never been sent.

To My Love,

I am counting down the days myself until we are married. I cannot wait to call you my husband and to wake to you every day of my life. I went over to Susie's today, and she showed me the wedding dress she is making for me. I still cannot believe she is giving us such a generous gift; it will be 3 months in July that she has worked so hard on it. I do hope that it does not disappoint you, although I find it rather grand. It will go perfectly with the blue ribbon that you gave me. I am so very lonely here without you; nothing feels the same without you to share it all with. I am, however, very proud of what you have accomplished. You are truly the knight in shining armor. I hope that God keeps you safe and returns you home to me soon.

All My Love, Your Mary

Ugh! I can't, this is so gut-wrenching to read. Anna thought to herself, feeling like she was imposing by reading all these private letters. However, Anna also knew she didn't have another option. She had already decided on this fate, and she had to plow on to get through the other docs.

After reading through the last of the letters from Benjamin, Anna could fully appreciate and understand the love that the couple shared together—it was deep, passionate, and infinite love. Anna gained some understanding as to why Mary could never have given up hope.

The last document she found was a little difficult to read. The black ink on the page had smeared across some of the paper. Then, she realized it was another military document, the letter notifying Mary that Benjamin had gone missing in action during the Battle of Gettysburg on July 3rd, 1863. Anna shuddered at the words on the page. "Oh god," Anna sighed. Anna took a photo of this document also for reference before tucking it away back into the box. Placing the box on the top shelf of her closet, Anna wanted to ensure that it was hidden from prying eyes and that her mom or dad wouldn't find it.

Rubbing her sleepy eyes, which felt strained at this point, Anna laid back on her bed and briefly fell back asleep until an incoming text message woke her.

"Sounds great. Y are u awake so early babe? x"
"Had weird dream & decided to read Mary's docs."
"Can't wait to hear about it! Wish I cud have been with u."

"Me 2. Cafeteria @ 7:30?"

Anna then realized that it was now 6:30. "Lord, I am going to have to put some anti-puff cream on these shopping bags," Anna snorted at herself. *Hmm, better let my parents know I'm going to school early.*

With that in mind, Anna ran downstairs to tell her mom that she would be leaving soon. "Morning, darling, you're up early," her mom smiled.

"Yeah, I'm going into school early today, if that's okay? I'm going to meet Boston in the cafeteria before class."

"Wow, you guys are becoming quite the item! Yes, you can go, but don't make a habit of meeting up with him before class, okay?" Her mom smiled as she clasped Anna's face with her hands.

"Thanks, Mom, I won't. Thank you sooo much!" Anna replied excitedly.

Anna quickly jumped in the shower and threw on her jeans, white hoodie, and brown leather knee-high flat boots. "Bye Mom. Thanks again—bye pups!" Anna shouted as she left through the garage door to her car.

It was a frosty, crisp morning. Anna admired the frost-covered trees as she drove to school. Her phone buzzed—it was Abbey.

"Hey Abs!"

"Hey, so, meeting lover boy for an early morning romantic

meal? You two can't seem to keep away from each other!"

"Whatevs! I just wanted to see him—I read through some stuff last night, and it just made me feel weird and miss him. I'll tell you all about it later today. Sorry for the last-minute bail on your guys' car ride to school. I'm really sorry. It won't happen again, promise!" Anna said apologetically.

"Oh no worries, Anna, we can handle one day without a ride. Besides, my mom is going to let me take her car to school today, which is pretty cool. It's been a while since I could drive myself. Anyway, I'll let you go. Tell lover boy I said hi," Abbey joked before hanging up.

Anna pulled up to school. It was nice that she was able to park so close to the front door. The parking lot was almost empty at that time in the morning. Only the students who were enrolled in early bird classes were there. Anna grinned as she saw Boston's black Mustang parked and took the spot right next to it. "Hmmm" Anna pursed her lips. *I can't wait to give you a big kiss, Mr. Tate!*

Boston looked up from his phone as he sat at one of the tables in the empty cafeteria looking like a young Greek god, his big brown eyes fixated on Anna as she walked toward him. Anna still found it hard to believe that he was all hers.

"Hey, how you doin' cupcake?" Boston joked in his best mobster impression.

"Hey yo!" Anna giggled back. "Ha ha! You're in a goofy mood," Anna sat down and kissed Boston gently.

"Hmm, what do you expect? My girl wants to have breakfast with me. What better way to start my day!" He ran his finger gently through her hair. "You look absolutely gorgeous today. Well obviously... well, you always do," he added as Anna raised her eyebrows at him as she sat down on the stool in front of him. "So, tell how come you were you up so early this morning?" he asked inquisitively.

Anna proceeded to tell Boston everything that had happened during the wee hours of the morning. "Incredible, yet slightly disturbing. It's weird 'cause I can imagine how Benjamin must have felt being away from Mary and not being able to see her." Boston suddenly realized what he had just let slip out. He squirmed slightly with embarrassment.

Anna sat quietly for a minute, squealing with excitement and doing a happy dance in her head but trying to stay cool and appear to not make a big deal out of it. "Anna, listen, I hope I'm not making you feel rushed about us. It's just that I can't to seem to play it cool with you, and I don't want to pretend to. I think about you all the time, even when I'm at football practice getting tackled. I can't seem to get you out of my mind. Let me know if—"

"Boston," Anna interrupted, "Don't worry. I don't feel rushed, honestly. I feel the exact same way about you. I just want to be with you all the time, and when I'm not with you, I really miss you. Honestly, it scares the hell out of me how much I care about you so soon."

"Well, I'm relieved to hear you say that. I wish we could just hang out together today instead of sitting in class," Boston leaned across the table and held Anna's hand.

"Hmm, me too. This morning when I woke up from my dream, all I wanted to do was talk to you or see you," Anna grinned.

"You can talk to me any time you want. And I seriously mean any time."

"You're so sweet." Anna leaned in and smiled, anticipating what was going to follow that comment. Boston kissed Anna softly and then burning with excitement his tongue found hers as he kissed her more deeply. Every nerve in her body tingled with excitement, especially now, knowing he felt the same way.

"Now let's go eat. As usual, I'm starving." Boston abruptly pulled away from Anna and tugged her to her feet.

CHAPTER SEVENTEEN

"So, Anna, what the hell happened last night or this morning?! Did you read through any more of the papers in that box?" Abbey grabbed Anna's arm in anticipation.

In some strange way, Anna felt like she was gossiping about Mary after she showed Anna where to look, but at the same time, Anna owed Abbey and Jay an explanation of the truth after they risked their necks to essentially help Mary.

"I need to get to class. But tell Jay to meet us by the bleachers at lunch, and I'll tell you both all about it," Anna relented.

"Fair enough," Abbey conceded.

The morning passed quickly for Anna as she tried to concentrate on her classes and let her mind rest from all the extra-curricular activities. The last thing she needed was for her schoolwork to slip and jeopardize her graduation plans. A loud crack of thunder made Anna practically jump out of her seat. "Jesus!" she exclaimed as the rest of the classroom turned around and laughed. Anna could feel her cheeks turning a rosy shade as the embarrassment flooded her body.

"A little jumpy this morning, aren't we, Ms. Ipswich," Mrs. Alequinn noted as she also turned her attention toward Anna.

"So sorry... I guess so. The thunder was super loud," Anna said apologetically.

"No need to worry, Ms. Ipswich, just checking into make sure you're still breathing," Mrs. Alequinn said sarcastically. She was a very thin, pale woman with platinum wavy hair that was always pulled back into a bun. Peering over her large black framed glasses, Mrs. Alequinn looked almost too cool for school or maybe even for ice, or so she seemed to think.

Mrs. Alequinn was one of the less popular teachers at school, due to her demeaning and sarcastic nature. It almost seemed like Mrs. Alequinn enjoyed making her students feel uncomfortable, like the school day was one big power trip for her. Her feedback in class wouldn't necessarily be classed as 'constructive criticism,' and more like someone needed to purchase her one of those 'dummy' stamps. Anna could feel herself resisting as hard as she could not to roll her eyes. Luckily, class ended shortly after her embarrassing moment of the day.

"Ugh, my god! I cannot stand that woman!" Anna said, slamming her locker door shut after switching out books between classes.

"Anna—chill out! I've never seen you so fired up before," Boston was both amused and surprised.

"Whatevs. At the end of the day, Boston, she is a teacher, and she should try acting like one, instead of trying to play cool and so, so sophisticated all the time. Really, she acts like a mean girl picking on her students. I swear she's like an older version of Brianna, or maybe she should legally change her name to Regina George!" Anna snarled back.

"Jeez... I'm sorry." Boston cracked a smile. "Meow... I kinda like the feisty side of you," Boston said, wrapping his arm around Anna's waist and pulling her in tightly.

Phew, Anna thought to herself as a tingle went down her spine. Anna giggled as she felt her body relax from Boston's bear hug. "I think I'm just overly tired. I wish we didn't have class... Will you be able to meet us at bleachers for lunch?" Anna frowned playfully at Boston.

"Don't tempt me... it wouldn't take much for you to be a bad influence on me." Boston rested his forehead on Anna's and breathed in sharply. "Come on... we need to get to class. I'll see you for lunch at the bleachers," he smiled and pulled away.

During lunch, Anna filled Abbey and Jay in on the information she had read and showed them the pictures.

"No wonder you wanted to get to school early today. That's just so sad. It had to make you feel weird. Anna, now that you have some more information, when will you actually start to research more on Benjamin?" Abbey said, handing the phone back to Anna.

"I'm going to start when I get home tonight. There are some websites I found that I think could be a good starting point, sites that are dedicated to the soldiers who served during the war. You can search by their name and regiment and it provides you with some data on them. I guess I'll begin my search there. I doubt it's going to be super easy though, otherwise other people would have found out what happened to Benjamin by now."

"Other people didn't have Mary helping them or have the information you have now," stated Jay.

"Yeah, that's true," Anna agreed.

"Let me know if you need help with anything, Anna. Use me at your will," Abs smiled.

"Now I like the sound of that!" laughed Jay

"You're such a disgusting pig, Jay, really." Abbey tried to hide the laughter on her face. Boston couldn't help himself. He high-fived Jay. "Don't encourage him, Boston," added Abbey.

Boston sat next to Anna on the bleacher and put his arm

around her shoulder. "So how would you like to come for dinner at my house? I don't have practice tonight."

"Hmm, tempting. Let me make sure my parental units are cool with it. I do want to do some research tonight, so I could go home first for an hour and then come over?"

"Cool, sounds good! Let me know what your mom says." Boston planted a small peck on Anna's cheek as she began texting her mom.

"Mom, you ok with me going 2 Boston's for dinner 2night?"

"Wow, you're seeing him again already?! Yes, but remember your curfew, so don't be late, and I do think you need to spend some time at home tomorrow night, ok? You've been out the last few days... x"

"I get it Mom. I won't be going out tomorrow. Thanks! I Love You x"

"She's fine with it. I'll come over about 5:30 then," Anna smiled.

After dinner, Boston and Anna headed up to his bedroom, so they could watch a movie together. Boston had a lot of football memorabilia in his room. Photos, awards, and a football jersey decorated the dark-blue walls. Two big skylights were placed in the center of the room with a small desk underneath them. Boston's queen size bed covered with a gray plaid comforter lay opposite of a dark brown chocolate leather sofa on the other side. A TV and an Xbox sat on a table across from the sofa. "This is a really cool-looking room. I love the giant skylights," Anna commented.

"Thanks, I think it's pretty cool. My parents converted the attic into a room for me... Dad says he's going to turn it into his media space when I leave for college," Boston laughed. "I like being on the third-floor 'cause it's more private, and it means they can use the spare bedrooms below for guestrooms and offices. It was actually my idea to have my own floor, but it worked out well for them too."

"And do you get everything you want, Mr. Tate?" teased Anna.

"No, but because they are out all the time, it makes things a little easier." Boston laughed.

Anna sat down on the leather couch, as Boston pulled a throw blanket from the shelf in his closet. "Here, you look chilly," he said, tossing it onto the couch beside her.

"I am a little chilly, but then again I'm always cold" she smiled. Boston sat down next to her and turned on the television and XBOX.

"Want to watch a movie on Netflix?"

"Sure, that sounds good. Whatever you want to watch is fine with me."

"OK, how about *Love Actually*... that's kind of a holidays-type movie, right?"

"I l-o-v-e that movie. Definitely a classic," Anna replied, surprised at his thoughtful girly chick-flick pick.

Boston laid his head on the cushion and gently leaned Anna in toward him. Stretching his body out across the couch, she laid down next to him as the film started. *Oh my god... oh my god...!* Anna thought to herself excitedly. *I can't wait to tell Abs that we spooned for the first time today!* she smiled to herself triumphantly.

They watched the movie quietly for about 30 minutes until Boston broke the silence. "So, how did the research go? Find anything interesting?"

"It went okay. Benjamin's name did come up in the online database, but it just said that he went missing in action. The regiment information lined up with what was on the paperwork, which is good—not that I doubted it, but at least it proves its authenticity. But no other details than that so far."

"I have an idea. How would you like it if we drove to Gettysburg for lunch on Saturday and we can stop by the history museums and talk to some folks about how we can find out more about Benjamin?"

"Oh, Boston, wow... that would be great! I would love that!" Anna smiled.

"Great! We should probably leave at around 10 o'clock Saturday morning, so I can come pick you up then?" he said with a well-deserved grin on his face.

"Sure, I'll just need to let my parents know, but let's plan on that. I still can't believe that we've only been together for a month and a half, it seems like so much longer." Anna rested her head back down on his shoulder.

"I know, it feels like we've been together for a year or 10... sheesh! Or maybe it's been a year or so of flirtatious foreplay," Boston joked.

"Hey, that's mean!" Anna pouted, pulling her head away from him. Boston wrapped his arms around her tightly, pulling her back toward him and laughing. He leaned his head down to kiss her.

"Umm, wish I could just lay here with you all night," he said in between kisses.

Anna sighed. "I wish I could too," she replied as her stomach tightened. She mingled her fingers in with Boston's hair as they continued to kiss. The kisses deepened as her hands glided slowly up and down Boston's arms and back. Boston's hands caressed her face, hair, and then made their way down to the top of her thighs and around to her butt. Anna let out a moan as she squeezed his bicep. Once again, Boston pulled away as they both panted like dogs who just came inside from the heat. "What's wrong, why did you stop?" she almost begged Boston.

"I have so much respect for you, Anna. As much as I want honestly to rip your top off, we need to take it slow. I don't want to eff anything up." Boston bit his bottom lip as if he was trying to control himself.

"Listen, I'm not trying to rush into anything here myself, but I think we can take it slow while still having fun at first base, right?"

Anna tried her best not to sound annoyed.

Boston let out an exasperated sigh, "I mean, I guess you're right, babe. I'll try."

"Listen, Boston, if you're not into this, I don't want to force you to make-out with me or put your hand up my shirt. I can just leave now if it's—"

"Jesus, Anna! Do you realize how freakin' attracted I am to you? I've never felt this way before about anyone. You have no idea how many thoughts I have about you that run through my head multiple times a day. Trust me, no one is forcing anyone here; it's self-preservation. I'm trying to be a gentleman because I don't want things to move too fast and get complicated. I'm just trying to be respectful of you." This was the first time that Anna had seen Boston get upset.

Anna leaned in closer to Boston. "Please don't be mad. I love that you want to respect me. Honestly, I do. But I have needs too. Don't you think that I'm daydreaming about those exact things too? I'm not suggesting that we have sex tomorrow, but I need you, Boston. I need to feel close to you, and I'm telling you that it's okay to take things a little further. I need to feel more of you Boston, and I want you to feel more of me."

Boston didn't hesitate. He grabbed Anna's face with both hands and kissed her more deeply than he had before. Anna leaned back gently onto the leather couch, pulling Boston with her. The couple touched each other in ways that they had promised, keeping it PG 13 for what seemed like hours. Both Anna and Boston felt some sense of relief from their pent-up tension, and a newfound closeness that they hadn't possessed before. After they finished their 45-minute make-out session, they watched *That 70s Show* and giggled together, while just cuddling on the couch.

Anna woke to Boston stroking her hair gently. "Hey sleepy head, you need to wake up. You need to make sure you get home before curfew, so you don't get into trouble with your parents."

Anna squinted as she slowly opened her eyes; "Hmmm," she moaned, stretching her arms up. Then Anna sharply snapped back into reality, "Wait! Oh my god, did I fall asleep?! I'm so sorry, Boston, that was super lame of me. What time is it?!" Anna sat up quickly, embarrassed.

"It's okay, you're not late, and really, don't worry about it. I know how tired you must be, and without the risk of sounding a little stalkerish, you looked really beautiful sleeping. I quite liked you sleeping on me," Boston replied softly and honestly.

"You are so sweet. You really need to be careful talking to girls that way. They're liable to fall in love with you," Anna smirked with all sincerity.

"I don't talk to girls that way, Anna, just to you," Boston replied seriously as he looked directly into Anna's eyes.

Oh my god, is he implying... no... is he? Well, I think I am falling in love with Mr. Tate. Not that I'll be the first one to say—heck no!

Anna thought to herself. Shocked by the serious tone of his response, words failed her momentarily. Anna responded by kissing Boston gently, but with the conviction of her thoughts. Unable to verbalize yet just how much he meant to her; she told him via a kiss.

Boston groaned, "Ugh, god, you better go before I convince you otherwise, babe." Boston struggled to pull back and resist the urge to continue kissing her for the next three hours. "Just think, we have Thanksgiving break coming up in 5 days, and we'll have a full week off school together."

"Hmm, I'm not sure I could see you every day for a whole week," Anna teased.

The next morning, Anna picked Abbey up from her house on the way to school. Abbey was super excited when Anna told her what Boston had said the night before.

"Oh-my-god-Anna, I think he's in LOVE with you! Or falling for you at the very least. I've never had a guy speak to me that way before. You are so lucky! Awww, you guys will have the cutest kids ever, live in the cutest designer home with a dog and an iron fence... the whole thing!"

"Woah, woah, woah! Settle down, Abs. I'm seventeen. I'm not in any rush to pop out babies, thank you very much," Anna giggled. "I don't want to end up on the next season of *Teenage and Pregnant*."

"Obviously not, smarty pants. But... you know... down the line, could you picture yourself marrying him a few years from now? Can you picture yourself, Mrs. Boston Tate? Ha ha!"

"You're such a dork, Abs. But... maybe," Anna squealed in excitement, "Seriously though, it's only been like two months. That would be a lotta years from now." Anna contemplated as they pulled up to Jay's house. "Never say never, I guess," Anna replied coolly.

CHAPTER EIGHTEEN

Once Anna arrived home from school, she started thinking about Jay's suggestion of checking the hiding spot at the Mack house for the key. Anna would love nothing more to get her hands on that key and be able to keep others out from making a mockery of Mary. It had been a couple of days since she was last at the house, so Anna decided that she would go there that night, after the house closed for the day, and check to see if anyone had replaced the key in the hiding spot.

Anna had promised her mom the night before that she would spend some time at home instead of going out with Boston or her friends again. There was a small window of time between when the Mack House would finally be empty and when her mom would want her seated at the table and ready for dinner at 6:30. The Mack House wouldn't close until 5 p.m., and then Anna would need to buffer in some small amount of time to ensure that the Historical

Society members had cleaned up, put their brochures and stuff away, and had actually left the parking lot before she could attempt to search for the key. Anna settled on going to the Mack House at 6 p.m. This would give her 5 or 10 minutes to search around for the key, and she would at least feel somewhat hidden, as it would also be completely dark out by that time. The dark would give her some level of coverage from any random people driving along 106 at that time of night.

Anna did need to figure out what to tell her mom. Since she worked from home most of the time, Anna would need some explanation for popping out in the evening. *Hmmm, what would make her the least suspicious? I don't want her thinking I'm sneaking out to meet up with Boston or anyone.* "Hey Mom! I'm a freakin' idiot and just realized that I left my laptop in Abbey's backpack."

"How did you manage to do that?" asked her mom.

"Well, I had Phys Ed today, and during that same period Abs realized that she left her laptop in her locker. So rather than going all the way up to the third floor to come back down to her science class on the first floor, I just let her borrow mine. Abbey was already running late to begin with, so she really didn't have time. I obviously didn't need it for P.E. Seriously, sometimes she's the smartest ditz I know, LOL," Anna laughed, she was pretty proud of the on-the-fly story she came up with.

"That does sound like a hassle. I get it, just don't spend an hour picking up your laptop from her house. You know we're having some family time tonight, so make it snappy."

"Totally agree. I told her I'll be by her house at 6 'cause I wanted to take the dogs out on a quick walk, and she's doing some online tutoring thing anyway."

"Ok, honey, thanks for letting me know," her mom settled.

Anna kept to her word and took Shaggy and Tutu on a brief walk as the November evening air was extremely chilly. While walking back to her house, Anna decided that she may as well just quickly go search for the key on her own, at the Mack House, as there wasn't much point in asking Abbey, Boston, or Jay to meet her there for a five-minute task. Anna didn't want them to feel like she was leaving them out, especially now that they are all very much invested with the whole ordeal. Anna did think, however, that it was a good idea to tell them about her plans for the evening, just so they were aware. Anna sent a quick group text to her three closest friends.

"Hey guys! Wanted to let u know that I'm going to the Mack House @ 6 tonight 2 check for the key. Don't need any help, just wanted 2 let you know I'm going."

Abbey responded first, *"Anna, pick me up, I'll go with!"*

"No, it will take me 2 mins to check. I'll text y'all after and let u know if I find it."

Next, Boston tried, *"It's pretty dark there, not sure u shud be walking around by yourself. I can come meet u there."*

Jay added his opinion too; *"Abs and Boston are right, Anna."*

"Seriously guys, I'm not a toddler, LOL. Will b fine – promise. Will text u after. XX"

Abbey texted last for all of Anna's friends, *"OK. You better text us as soon as you are home! X"*

Anna shook her head in amusement at her overprotective friends and boyfriend. *Gotta love em,* she thought to herself.

5:55 p.m. rolled around finally after Anna checked her watch for the twentieth time. Anna let her Mom know she was leaving to go to Abbey's, tilted her head to the fresh air outside, and climbed into her car. *It's freakin' freezing out here!!!* She shuddered to herself while turning on her electric seat warmers and setting her car's heater to the highest temperature setting possible. Anna headed to the Mack House while listening to her latest Audible book she was obsessed with, *The Legend of The Rochesters,* which was a young adult book about a very wealthy and popular family based in Boston, Massachusetts. A good audible book always helped Anna get out of her own headspace and relax.

When Anna arrived in the parking lot at the Mack House, she hadn't prepared herself for just how creeped out she would feel. Being at the old house by herself, in the dimly lit parking lot, and being surrounded by almost complete darkness with not another house in site, Anna began to slightly regret her decision to not drag Abbey or someone along with her for support. Anna's mind started to race through a bunch of 'what if' scenarios. What if an axe murderer or some weirdo was hiding in the trees behind the house just waiting for some idiotic teenage girl to wander around in the freakin' dark by herself and pounce on her? Or, what if a stranger comes along the road, sees her walking around alone, and kidnaps her? The list went on. *What in the heck were you thinking, Anna? You are a moron!*

The wind suddenly picked up and started to make some faint howling sounds as it blew across the branches on the many trees that surrounded the small home. Feeling completely creeped out now, Anna hightailed it over to the main steps in front of the Mack House. Feeling around with one hand in the hiding spot under the stairs, Anna moved as quickly as she could, using the other hand to shine her phone's flashlight in the dark space. Anna couldn't feel anything. "Damn it!" she growled in frustration. Anna felt again, digging around with her fingers into the smallest of nooks and crannies. "Wait, wait," Anna said out loud as her fingers touched a small piece of cold metal.

Finally, Anna found what she was looking for. "Wahooooo!!" she screamed out loud. Anna was over the moon that she finally had the key.

Anna triumphantly began walking away from the house and toward her car. Stopping in her tracks, and she suddenly saw headlights from the road coming into the parking lot. *OMG, OMG! Here we go, I'm gonna get kidnapped!* She panicked.

As the car stopped in a parking spot, she could make out that there were four people in the car, but the darkness covered their faces. Then, the interior light flicked on as the driver's door began opening. "Holy shit," Anna said when she realized who was in the car: Brianna, Mark, Syreena, and Braidon. Anna guessed that Brianna finally browbeat Syreena into coming to the Mack House, seeing as she wasn't able to go the last time. Although, Syreena seemed excited to come and try out the legend for herself as she giggled along with Brianna. Anna started walking back toward her car a little quicker this time and put the key she found in her zipper pocket.

"Well, well, well, look who we have here!" Brianna smirked. "What on earth are you are doing out here? Chasing ghosts, Anna?" she hissed.

Anna really had no good excuse, and, well, she sure as hell wasn't going to tell Brianna the one reason. Thinking quickly, Anna replied, "Umm, no. Boston and I came here the other day when the Historical Society had the house open. I dropped one of my favorite earrings and just realized it a few hours ago, so I came to check the parking lot." *Not too bad*, she thought to herself.

"Oh really, not sure I believe that. When you came here with me, you seemed to believe that Mary was talking to you. It was SO crazy!" Brianna laughed.

"Brianna, as I recall, you thought you heard and saw some

weird shit too. So, it seems to me like maybe you just got scared and didn't fully realize what was going on," Anna retorted.

"Are you getting upset that I'm talking about your new bestie, Mary, Anna? I mean really, isn't she a bit too old to be friends with you?" Brianna didn't realize that she was stepping into sensitive territory for Anna.

"Grow up, Brianna, you sound ridiculous. I'll admit, I thought I heard her say something, but that doesn't mean she actually did. It was a weird night, but isn't that why you took us there? Isn't that what you wanted? And, in fact, isn't that why the four of you are here again? I guess you just enjoy tormenting practically everyone." Brianna was taken aback. She wasn't used to people standing up to her, and she really didn't have a good comeback.

"Whatevs. Anyway, aren't you and Boston just becoming quite the little couple? Syreena, Braidon, you guys know the famous Anna, right? Well, if you didn't before, I'm sure you do now that Anna is dating up in life," Brianna scoffed. Brianna couldn't embarrass Anna over the Mary stuff, so now she decided to make it more personal.

Dating up... Anna thought to herself. *What an egotistical little madam!*

"Yes... Anna, how are you?" Syreena said coolly. Braidon just remained quiet and nodded his head at Anna. Mark and Braidon just looked uncomfortable but equally remained silent. Anna didn't bother to answer Syreena. She knew full well that Syreena was one of Brianna's Barbie doll groupies and had no real interest in who she was.

"'Dating up...' That's an interesting way to put it, Brianna. Boston might feel like he's the one dating up after the last girlfriend he had." Anna wasn't about to let Brianna demoralize her. The girl is a big enough bully at school to others, but she would stand up for herself. Boston had dated Brianna's best friend, Bethany, for about six months the past spring semester. Boston broke it off with her because she became way too attached too soon, and Boston just wasn't that into her. Brianna was none too happy when Boston ended things. It was very inconvenient for her social calendar when the four of them had to stop going out on double dates all the time. If everyone hadn't already got the memo, it's Brianna's world and everyone else is just living in it. Bethany also wasn't the most pleasant girl. She was a Brianna wannabe, so it wasn't a huge surprise to anyone when it didn't work out.

"Ugh! Be careful, Anna. That's my best friend you're talking about there. Seriously, you want to throw insults about Bethany when you're the one looking a little crazy being out here in the dark all by yourself at the Mack House, of all places. People are going to find this story super strange when I tell everyone at school tomorrow. Little miss priss thinks she's a ghost hunter!" Brianna chuckled and Syreena followed suit.

"Bri—come on, let's just get going with this stuff if we're going to do it," Mark chimed in, seemingly trying to help Anna by breaking up the situation.

"Mark—don't interrupt!"

"Brianna—let's just make this clear. I could care less what you think about me, or what immature, unfounded rumor you want to try to spread about me at school. In fact, this whole conversation is super ridiculous. I'm leaving. You all have a good night!" Anna said as she took a step toward her car. But Brianna blocked her from moving farther.

Brianna's face, now looking screwed up, got closer to Anna's. "No, miss thing. I'm going to make this clear to you! You don't belong in my circle, and Boston is way too good for you. He's one of our star players, for Christ's sake! One day soon, he's going to wake up and realize that, and will kick you to the curb when he remembers that he fits in with us and not with you. You... you... are no one, Anna!"

Anna felt perturbed by Brianna's anger toward her. She knew all along that Brianna could be a nasty, selfish, arrogant person, but she had no idea that she could be this much of a bitch with this type of temper. Although Anna was getting madder by the second at the horrible things Brianna was saying about her and Boston, she was also concerned about how enraged Brianna became and the fact that she's by herself while Brianna had three friends with her. Anna was not someone who had any interest in getting into a physical altercation, it's just not her. There's standing up for yourself, and there's knowing when it's time to leave. *Be the bigger person, Anna. Brianna needs to cool down*, she coached herself. *Is Brianna that jealous of my relationship with Boston, to get this mad? You would think that Boston had broken up with her*, Anna thought to herself.

"Bri, calm down babe. Why are you getting so upset, just chill and get inside," Mark tried to intervene again as he grabbed her hand and tried to pull her away. Brianna just stood in her same spot, nostrils flared and lips pursed, just staring at Anna.

Anna stayed still and didn't respond. She could feel that for the past 20 minutes, her phone had been vibrating in her pocket over and over with incoming text messages, but obviously she wasn't able to pay any attention to it.

One minute later, another car's headlights approached the parking lot, and everyone turned their attention to see who was coming. Anna felt her shoulders relax instantly when she realized it was Boston's Mustang. *How did he know to come here?* Anna thought to herself. Boston quickly parked his car and got out.

"What the hell is going on here? Why are you guys just standing around?" As Boston assessed the situation, he could tell something was very wrong by the look on Anna's face, and by the look on Brianna's. "Is someone going to answer me? What hell is going on??"

"Your girlfriend needs to learn to watch her mouth," Brianna snapped back. Anna looked on the edge of tears at this point, emotionally exhausted from Brianna and the sheer relief of Boston showing up.

"The girls were kinda getting into it, Boston. I tried to break it up a couple of times, but I was ignored," Mark fessed up. This was the first time that Brianna was mute. She knew that Boston would be angry when he found out how she had treated Anna.

"Boston, I'd really rather just leave... please." Anna felt like she wanted to combust but refused to let Brianna or the others see her cry.

"Mark, I'd like to go home... now!" Brianna demanded quietly.

"I get it, let's go guys," Mark said as he unlocked his SUV and motioned for the three of them to get in.

"Anna, we've been texting you for like 25 minutes, and you didn't respond. What have you been doing? I really want to know what went on here. Abs, Jay, and I thought something was wrong. You can't even imagine the freakin' scenarios running through my head," Boston said concerned.

Anna looked down at her phone, waiting for Mark's car to pull out of the parking lot. The second they were gone, she felt tears begin falling down her cheeks. "God, I feel like all I do anymore is cry around you, and I'm not a crier," she said as he put his arms around her, holding her tight.

"Come on, you must be freezing. Come sit in my car, and we can talk in the warmth," he said, kissing her forehead.

Anna divulged everything that happened and everything that was said to her about Boston. "I can't freakin' believe her! I knew

Brianna could be a brat and at times be snarky, but I had no idea she had that kind of anger. You know she's full of shit, right? I feel lucky every day that I'm with you Anna. You're smart, funny, beautiful... you're amazing! I've had it with Brianna and her circle crap! Well, she can consider me no longer in it. If Mark wants to hang with her, I can't stop him. But I want nothing to do with her. I'm so, so sorry, babe, that you had to deal with that. Really, I am," Boston said while leaning in and giving Anna another big hug.

"Thanks for coming and for talking me down, Boston. I love how protective you are of me. It really means a lot. You really mean a lot to me. From now, on I'm just going to straight up ignore her. She's such a negative person, and I don't need that in my life. Not when I have such a great family, friends, and a boyfriend to focus on." Anna unzipped her pocket. "Ohhh, looky what I found?" she said as she pulled out the key.

"Awesome, you found it! Well, that's gotta make you feel good, knowing that people like Brianna won't be able to bother Mary anymore."

"After tonight, it makes me feel even better," she said while leaning in and kissing him.

"Listen, you're gonna get in trouble 'cause you're super late getting home for dinner. Let me follow you home, 'cause you're upset and I want to make sure you make it there alright."

"You're so sweet," Anna beamed back. "I need to think of a good excuse though. My mom is going to be super pissed at me," she frowned.

Anna and Boston pulled up in her driveway. Anna got out of her car and quickly walked over to Boston's window. "Thanks again for what you did tonight. I really do appreciate it," she said, leaning in and giving him a quick goodnight kiss.

"Anytime, babe," Boston replied. "I better get out of here so you can get inside and see your parents," he said while shifting his car in reverse. "Text me before bed," he said as he slowly began to reverse.

Anna glanced at her watch. Dinner started 40 minutes ago, and she knew her mom would be upset. Feeling all kinds of guilty, Anna walked into her house. When Anna got inside, her mom came walking up to the front door. "Anna, what took you so long? And where have you been? I tried to call you," she said frustrated. But then as she took a closer look at Anna's face, she could tell clearly that something was wrong. "What's wrong with you?" she asked more softly.

"Nothing, Mom. It's not a big deal." Thinking fast on her feet, she replied, "Abs and I just had a disagreement."

"Oh, honey, so that's why you're late. Come on, let's go eat dinner. Then we can go watch some Bravo, and you can catch me up on how you and Boston are doing," she said while giving Anna's arm a gentle squeeze. Anna felt a pang of guilt run through her. This wasn't like Anna to hide things and lie to her mom. *I hate this.*

I wish I could tell Mom about everything... about Mary and what happened with Brianna tonight. Humpf, maybe I just need to tell her what's going on and hope that she will understand, Anna thought to herself.

"Sure. I just need to run potty real quick, and I'll be right back," replied Anna. Anna ran upstairs and put the key to Mary's home in the same box with Mary's other belongings, tucked away safely.

CHAPTER NINETEEN

S itting in history class during third period, Mr. Richardson continued his discussion on the history of Cannon Falls and the Battle of Gettysburg. Mr. Richardson talked about the story of the only civilian casualty during the civil war. Mary Virginia "Jennie" Wade, a poor young woman of 20 years old, who was standing in her kitchen when a stray bullet came straight through the walls of her home, killing her. As Anna sat thinking of Jennie's tragedy, her mind swayed back to Mary's tragedy of her lost love and her current situation.

Why me? How is this even happening to me that I am communicating with Mary and now with Benjamin? Anna thought to herself as she reflected on the entire situation. Anna decided she wasn't going to keep secrets from her mom any longer and that it was time to talk to her about it... and maybe, just maybe, her mom could shed some light on her situation. Anna knew that she needed to pick the right time to bring this up; when she can be alone with her mother. She decided to ask her mom to grab a hot tea and take the dogs on a walk to the park together. Anna texted her mom and made the plans.

Anna grabbed Abbey right before lunch, as she couldn't shake the conversation that played in her head on repeat from history class. "Ugh, we were told in history class about the only civilian casualty of the civil war, and it's just made me feel super weird."

"Well, doll, I hate to break it to you. You've been weird since the day I met you, LOL," Abbey giggled.

"You're so hilarious, Abs. Where can I buy my ticket for your next stand up?" Anna nudged Abbey's arm. "On a serious note, though, one thing that I have been thinking about a lot recently, particularly since reading through those letters, is how and why me? Why am I able to communicate with Mary? It's all so strange, and maybe it would make more sense if I had these types of experiences before, but I haven't."

"I get it, and, honestly, I couldn't even begin to guess, Anna. I know you've not been telling your mom about this stuff, but maybe you need to. Maybe she can help explain why this is happening," Abbey replied.

"Yeah, well, exactly. I felt super guilty last night about lying to my mom. I am a little concerned about what she might say or if she'll get mad or how she'll be about it all. But, I'm probably going to end up telling her about it at some point anyway. You know it's hard for me to keep secrets from her."

"Exactly," replied Abbey supportively.

Anna called Boston on her way home from school to tell him her plans, after she had dropped Jay and Abbey off. "Wish me luck! I'll text you later tonight to figure out plans to go to Gettysburg over Thanksgiving break. I forgot that I made plans with my mom for Saturday afternoon to help get the house ready for guests on Thanksgiving. The woman is super into decorating for the holidays. So if I skip, she'll be super pissed at me."

"I hear ya. No worries, just let me know how the conversation goes today and we can figure out the rest. I've gotta get to football practice. Later, babe!" Boston said before hanging up the call.

Anna felt anxious as she pulled into the driveway of her home, wondering how her mom will react—*will she think that I am joking or lying? Will she think that I am losing my mind?* Anna shook her head to shake off the pessimism and headed into her house. *Suck it up Anna. Just say 'eff it,' and it'll be okay.*

After quickly changing into her black Adidas yoga pants and putting on her most comfortable gray North Face hoodie, Anna ran downstairs and found her mom in the kitchen pouring a freshly brewed pot of Lavender Earl Grey tea mixed with milk and Stevia into matching pink Yeti mugs. "Hello, darling! Have a good day at school? I've got our tea ready and just need to get the leashes on the pups."

"Hey, Mom! Yeah, it was a pretty good day, it was... school. I'm just excited to get out in the fresh air and go on a walk. Rain poured down during PE class, so we had to stay inside and play volleyball in the gym. I'll grab Shaggy and Tutu and get them ready to go."

Anna and her mother walked quietly along a narrow path to the park, departing from the subdivision and leaving it behind them. They strolled past a lake that carried a light chilly breeze through the cloudy afternoon. Anna handed her tea to her mother to hold briefly while she pulled her hoodie up over her head to block the wind from the side of her face.

Anna's unusual silence did not go unnoticed by her mom. Looking over at Anna's face, she could tell that Anna was feeling anxious. "OK, lady, what is it? I can tell something is up with you, Anna, so spill," her mom smiled, nudging Anna's arm with her elbow.

Anna breathed in deeply. "OK, just please let me finish before you say anything? And I know, by the way, that what I'm about to say may sound, like, a little crazy, but let me just be clear that this is in no way a joke or a prank, and I'm being completely serious. I need you to believe me," Anna said, twisting Shaggy's leash around her hands and looping it around some of her fingers.

"Okay, I promise. But now you're worrying me." Her mom looped her arm through Anna's, encouraging her to go on.

Anna proceeded to tell her mom about her first visit to the Mack House, excluding the part about semi-breaking into the home at night. Anna continued to tell her about the yellow ribbons, the wooden box, and the vivid and surreal dreams she has had about Benjamin since the last time she visited the house.

Her mom kept her word and kept quiet, letting Anna divulge all the details.

Anna paused. "So, Mom, do you think I'm nuts now?"

"Wow! Anna, I—I'm just blown away," Anna's mom said, shaking her head. "I had no idea that firstly you had the ability to do that... anymore. And this whole thing that you are tied up in with Mary and Benjamin, it's... it's incredible! I don't know what else to say honey. I—"

Anna interrupted, "Wait! Wait. You just said," Anna signed in air quotes, "'anymore'; that I had the ability to do that anymore? What do you mean?" Anna said, her eyes wide in confusion and disbelief.

Stopping in her tracks, Anna's mom turned and put her hand

on Anna's upper arm and rubbed it gently. "Let's sit down on that bench over there and let the doggies run around, since we're the only ones here."

Anna and her mom walked over to the old, faded, gray wooden bench and unhooked the leashes from Shaggy and Tutu. The bench was one of many in the big open field of short grass, while trees and tall wild grass lined the field around them. A large kids play area consisting of swings, slides, and various climbing apparatus and ground completely covered in rubber mulch under the play equipment was on the other side of the open field, surrounded by a cedar fence.

Anna's mom sat down next to Anna on the bench and took a large sip of her warm tea. "When you were a little girl, and I'm talking when you were five years old, your dad and I were told by your Aunt Isabelle that she found you sitting up in your bed one night talking to someone. You had gone over to her house for a sleepover with your cousin Katie one night. Isabelle was walking past the bedroom that you were staying in on her way to bed when she overheard you. When she opened the door to check on you, you were sitting up in bed and talking. There was no one else in your room that your Aunt Isabelle could see. Isabelle asked what you were doing, and you told her that you were talking to the nice older boy sitting on the end of your bed. It really freaked your Aunt Isabelle out. Apparently, it was a pretty thorough conversation you were having."

"Mom, you are creeping me out right now!! I obviously don't remember any of this." Anna shuddered as multiple chills ran down her back.

Anna's mom squeezed her knee and continued. "Well, that night, Isabelle just shook it off, rationalizing the event as you dreaming and kinda sleepwalking, in order to get herself to sleep. But a couple of days later, she was still thinking about it. So much so, that she invited one of her neighbors over for a glass of wine, one who had lived in the neighborhood for a while. The neighbor also knew the previous owners of the home, so Isabelle hoped that once she told her neighbor what had happened, she might be able to provide some insight, if there was any insight to give."

Anna's mom paused and took in a deep breath before going on. "Isabelle said that her neighbor almost dropped her glass of wine straight onto Isabelle's brand-new carpet when Isabelle told her the story. The neighbor proceeded to then tell Isabelle that the previous owners were an older couple with four kids, three girls and one boy. The boy, the eldest, was in the military and died tragically during some exercise. He died at the age of 20."

"Mom!" Anna's exclaimed as her draw dropped.

"I know, honey. But that was the only thing like this that we experienced with you. Your dad and I never noticed anything else after that happen with you." Bu-ut, I should also tell you that your grandmother has the same gift, Anna. Knowing what you've told me today, you both are referred to as "sensitives."

"Grandma? Seriously? You and Dad have never told me anything about Grandma having some type of 'ability' or whatever you want to call it."

"Your grandmother is extremely private about these things. But I can tell you, without a shadow of a doubt, she has seen things that most people cannot see, including talking to people who have passed over. She does not want this to be common knowledge. In fact, she would be able to see mists appear by her bed when someone was trying to communicate with her."

"No way! I'm still surprised you guys never told me about this. I get it when I was younger, but now I'm seventeen," Anna said in disbelief.

"Well, again, your grandmother is very private and doesn't like to talk about it. But—there is more I should tell you," Anna's mom said, biting her lip.

"More? Seriously?!" Anna exclaimed. "My head is going to explode from all of this!"

"Yes. Buckle up, buttercup," Anna's mom said with a nod. "So, actually, you come from a long line of family members who are sensitive like you. Your grandmother wasn't the first, and you won't be the last. In fact, your ancestors dating back to the 1600s reported having this gift or capabilities in old diaries and passed down the information throughout the years to their children. Our Ipswich family migrated from England to Salem, Massachusetts, but then moved, or fled, from Salem in the early 1690s right around the time when the witchcraft accusations began. They were close friends with a very wealthy and influential council leader in Cambridge, Massachusetts, so your great-great-great-great-great-great-great-great-grandfather took a position on the council there so he and his family would be protected and avoid persecution."

"OMG, Mom, that is a-m-a-z! Can I google this stuff? I want to find out more about them. Does Dad know all about the family history? I mean, didn't he do 23 and Me, Ancestry, or something like that? This is totes unbelievable! I can't even...! Boston, Abbey, and Jay are going to totally freak out when I tell them this!" Anna's eyes were wide with excitement as she shook her head. Composing herself by pulling down her hoodie and patting it down around her neck, Anna then took a sip of tea. "So, I wonder though, if I had the ability when I was 5 and not since, why did it suddenly come back now? I mean, I guess I am always able to tell in a way if a place is haunted. But it seems like a lot of people can sense those types of things. But I just don't get why, 12 years later, I've suddenly become hyper-sensitive again, and particularly at Mary's house? It's just super strange."

"Well, I can't say for sure, Anna, but maybe it's because you've been thinking about a lot of big life changes recently, starting to think about colleges, a new boyfriend, and other new experiences. I imagine that all these experiences are just opening up your mind. Also, as you get older, you do become more in tune with your feelings. Your inner self has maybe woken up or bloomed."

Just then, a light wind gusted through, and Anna's mom caught a few stray strands of Anna's hair and tucked them behind her ears.

"You know, even though you're a mature seventeen-year-old, you're still my baby." Anna's mom chuckled while giving Anna a kiss on her cheek.

"Aww, Mom," Anna grinned. "I love you too. You're the best mom ever. This is just all super crazy. It's overwhelming at times, but I just know that I must help Mary. I'm communicating with her and now Benjamin, so I just have to trust that this is meant to be or fate or whatever you want to call it. Plus, as you know, I'm way too curious of a person and way too invested to stop now. I hope that's okay with you and that you don't want me to stop?"

"No, darling, of course not. I know this is obviously very important to you, and given everything you've told me; I think you should help. But just be careful! Don't let this part of your life become your whole life. You're seventeen, and you have a lot going on with school, your friends, and Boston; don't let this overwhelm you. Please let me know what you're doing and what you're up to, so I know that everything is okay." Anna's mom pulled her in for a big hug.

"Just don't lie to me about anything or shut me out. I feel better being in the know and that we can be honest with each other. You should definitely talk to your grandmother about this though. I really think she could help you in ways that I cannot. Also, we should tell your dad. It's not fair for him to be kept in the dark. If you want, I can mention something to him, unless you would rather do it?"

"I will, Mom. I promise. That would be great if you can talk to

Dad first, then I'll talk to him and answer any questions he might have." Anna squeezed her mom back reassuringly. Although this was a lot of information that Anna didn't fully expect, it made her feel reassured in knowing she isn't the only person in her family with this gift.

"It's gonna be dark soon. I'll get the leashes back on Shaggy and Tutu. I'm ready to get the doggies home and get some dinner. Telling your mom secrets is not always easy!" Anna joked. "Seriously though, this whole conversation and situation was mentally draining and I'm super hungry now!"

"Yes, we should. But just look at the gorgeous sunset, darling!" her mom pointed toward the sky above the treetops.

The sun was beginning to go down, and slowly the light began to fade while the pair sat on the bench. The sunset, a beautiful blend of blue, orange, and purple hues with grayish-white thin clouds stretched across the sky as if they were brush strokes on a canvas. The tall oak and fern trees splashed black silhouettes across the brilliant hues.

"That is really beautiful," Anna said as she pulled away from her mom's embrace. Anna stared intently at the almost witchy-looking sky; the moon faintly placed behind a wispy cloud. "Really looks magical, doesn't it," she said to her mom, looking around. Suddenly, Anna spotted something in the distance at the base of one of the grand oak trees. As Anna squinted her eyes harder to try and make out what it was, it became clear that the vision was a person. Anna's mouth nearly dropped open as the silhouette of a man, wearing what looked to be a uniform and a military hat, wandered around in the distance. "What the eff! Mom, do you see that over there?!" Anna exclaimed to her mom, pointing in the direction of the figure she saw.

"See what?" asked her mom inquisitively.

"The figure standing by the two oak trees, Mom. Right there!"

"No, honey, I don't see it. I just see the trees," her mom replied.

Anna let out a big sigh, shaking her head. As she looked back toward the trees again, the figure had vanished.

EPILOGUE
A sneak peek at the captivating conclusion of Miss Mary's story.

Anna called Abbey to tell her about the eye-opening, and scary, Simon encounter that happened earlier that day at the ancestry research center. Simon, a sophomore history student at Gettysburg College, seemed very knowledgeable about local history. Simon had been helping find artifacts and other historic documents that could have helped Abbey find out what happened to Benjamin. Unrealized by Anna before today, Simon had taken a special liking to her. He also found out that she and Boston were on a break, which created the perfect opportunity for him to make his move.

While working in a private room in the research center where the older books were kept, Simon settled in uncomfortably close to

Anna's face while she sat at the only wooden table in the room, deeply engrossed in the latest Cannon Falls history book she had found. Gently caressing her cheek with his warm fingers, he attempted to kiss her. Anna jumped to her feet immediately and pushed him away. "What are you doing, Simon?" Anna's stomach twisted in knots, as the sudden nervous heat made the air in the room feel thick.

"Come on, Anna, you know you want me," he smirked.

Anna very quickly attempted to walk away from Simon and headed toward the single exit door, but he grabbed her wrist and held it tightly. "Let go of me!" Anna yelled as she yanked her hand back, breaking free of him. "How dare you grab me like that! I never want to see you again! Lose my number, you creep!"

"Oh, don't you worry, babe, I never cared about Mary and Benjamin or this stupid investigation! I just didn't realize what a tightly wound little girl you are. I thought maybe we could have some fun together once you got rid of that pathetic high school boyfriend of yours." Simon spat through his teeth as his face flushed red with anger.

Anna decided it was best not to respond to Simon, as she left him at the entrance to the private room where he stood staring at her as she walked away. The realization came to her then that Simon was just trying to get his way with her all along. Helping her was just a way to get close, like a tiger stalking its prey. Anna began to nearly run out of the research center to her SUV, still feeling his fingers that landed on her waist as she had passed him. When in the safety of her vehicle with no turning back, she called Abbey right away.

When Anna finished sharing her unnerving story, Abbey returned only silence on the other end of the line at first, then broke her silence. "Well first off, I am so sorry, Anna, that happened to you, and second, I could literally kick that Simon's dumb ass for doing that to you."

"I know, what an absolute jerk! I never thought he would act like that. He seemed like such a sweet and helpful guy."

Anna later admitted that she had become completely obsessed, and if she was honest with herself, a little crazy over the Mary and Benjamin mystery.

"Listen Anna, I love you, you know that. But in being your best friend, I am entitled to tell you that I had noticed how you have been increasingly ignoring Boston as a result of all your research. Simon was clearly taking advantage of you and the situation. I never liked that asshole from the very beginning. Albeit this is a very admirable thing that you're trying to do for Mary, I totally get it, but you also must remember that you have your own life to live, and you must take care of number one—which is you. I'm not going to lecture you all day, Anna, but seriously, you need to call Boston and apologize. I know you love him, and he loves you too. Boston has looked completely miserable since you guys went on a hiatus from your relationship.

"I don't know, Abs, I feel like he hates me for what I've done, when all he did was try to be a good, supportive boyfriend. I'm such a fool!" Anna cried.

"I really think you broke his heart when you told him he's being selfish and that you needed to take a break. However, I honestly believe that you can work this out with him. Just be honest."

"Thanks, Abs. I just need to go right now and clear my head." Anna ended the call, replaying her more recent behavior toward Boston, how she had been ignoring him, not spending time with him, and now realizing that she had to own the fact that she was the one who had created a fracture in their relationship.

Anna had to see Boston in person, she couldn't run the risk of him just not answering or hanging up the phone on her. Anna made a sharp detour, turning down a small country road that would eventually lead to Boston's house. Consumed by guilt and regret, Anna started to cry harder, turning her cries into complete sobs. Moans poured out of her that she hadn't heard since she was a child as she sat wishing she could undo everything she had said and done to Boston a couple of weeks ago during their argument.

The rain suddenly turned into a torrential downpour and Anna could barely make out the road from the ditch between her windshield wipers barely being able to keep up with the rain and the tears flooding in her eyes. Anna quickly pulled her car to the side of the road in panic.

Barely able to control her breathing from the pure devastation she felt, Anna began to shake from crying so hard. Headlights appeared in her rearview mirror. All she could see was the blaze of yellow light through her rain-covered windows. The car continued to slowly creep up closer and closer to her car, Anna now feeling anxious for another reason.

Ugh, what are they doing? I hope they can see me in all this rain, she worried, remembering to turn her hazard lights on. Finally, the car came to a halt. Anna's heart pounded a million miles a minute, so fast that she felt like she could pass out. She watched with her eyes squinted, trying to focus on a figure that finally emerged from the driver's side door and began walking toward her car. Anna locked her doors and put her car into drive, pulling away very slowly in fear of the stranger. Suddenly, she heard the person knock on the back window and shout something, but the voice was muffled by the rain. Anna panicked, screaming, "Go away!" A familiar voice boomed back at her through the rushing sound of the downpour.

"Anna, wait! It's me!"

"Boston?!" Anna couldn't believe it.

"Anna, it's me! Stop and open the door!" he demanded, his voice sounding worrisome. Anna slammed her foot on the brake and put her car into park. She quickly opened her car door to see Boston standing there, soaking wet, his hair drenched and sticking like a frame around his beautiful face, which looked full of melancholy.

"Boston wha—how? How did you know where I was?" she said bewildered.

"The 'Friends App', remember? We enabled it on our phones a while back. Abbey texted me and told me that you were really upset and driving around, so I told her that I would look for you. Oh my god, Anna, I'm so sorry, please forgive me, baby?!" Boston begged. Anna couldn't tell if it was the rain or tears in his eyes making them look red.

"Boston, please, it's okay. I'm so sorry. I should have never said those things to you! I didn't mean any of it. I was just mad and trying to be a hurtful, selfish bitch. I love you so much!" Anna broke down in tears again and she got out of her car. She threw her head into Boston's chest, the familiar place that felt like home calming her uncontrollable sobs.

"Babe, please... I was the one being selfish. I don't even care about what we said to each other or that stupid argument. I just want to be with you. I can't handle being apart from you. I need you, Anna. I feel broken without you. I'm so mad at myself for starting that argument. You know that I love you more than anything. I should never have left you alone with Simon! I swear, he better hope he never runs into me. I'm going to fucking break that guy if I ever see him again!"

"Abbey told you about that already?! Simon is a total idiot; please just forget about him. I want to just focus on us and being happy together. I hated being apart from you too," she said, thrusting her lips onto him and kissing more deeply than she ever had before. Boston let out a low soft growl from the back of his throat. Anna could feel his body relax and give into her, and in return, her body gave into his.

Look for the concluding sequel to Miss Mary coming out soon, where Anna and friends continue their journey to unravel the mystery of Benjamin Watts' disappearance and attempt to bring peace to Miss Mary's tortured spirit.

Made in the USA
Middletown, DE
01 October 2023

39900523R00136